鄉民英文原來是醬!

Internet Slang

何志儒、陳怡歆◎著

鄉民用語老是掛在嘴邊……

你知道這一些「鄉民用語」的英文嗎？

Face off（踹共）

Count me in（+1）

Shitpost（廢文）

"Pics or it didn't happen"「沒圖沒真相」、"Chill、Passive"「佛系」、"Internet Troll"「網路小白」最夯英文網路用語！

你的鄰居和同學每天都在說的鄉民用語，隨處可見的流行語英文版！

台灣特有的PTT網路用語「懶人包」、「ㄈㄈ尺」、「幫高調」，每一個意思你都了解嗎？

Author's Preface → 作者序

這是一本活潑有趣的英語書籍，藉由網路鄉民用語，搭配相對應的英文片語和流行用語，讓讀者不僅可以透過了解現今網路上流行的中文用語，同時接觸相對應的生活化英文片語和俚語，並探討這些用語的起源及內涵。中西方在文化、語言上有差異，卻有諸多雷同之處，這就是語言和地球村奇妙之處。很開心能與大家分享這一本書，提供讀者用另一種方式學習英語；希望在有趣的閱讀下，為讀者在生活中帶來些許樂趣，並且有所獲益。

Christ 柯志儒

「這什麼？也太牛逼了吧？」，「真倒霉，躺著也中槍！」身為網路世代的子民，相信各位讀者肯定對這幾句話耳熟能詳。雖然我早就想撰寫類似的「本土化、超實用」英文書籍，但實際下筆後，才發現台灣鄉民的功力實在高深莫測，其精髓不是簡單用幾個英文字就能加以詮釋的。不過，「認真就輸了！」，就算被酸、被打臉，鄉民還是有自己的生存之道。希望讀者們讀完這一本書，除了閱讀這一本書覺得有趣以外，也能記下本書許多實用的英文句型和片語，別「神馬都是浮雲」才好喔！

Sunny 陳怡歆

Editor's Preface → 編者序

閱讀英文時，如果對閱讀的英文文章已經有基本的背景了解，或是有趣的主題都可以讓閱讀和學習時比較輕鬆愉快，透過閱讀是可以培養英文寫作能力和大大累積單字量。所以在企劃時刻意選擇最貼近台灣人、最夯的「鄉民用語」選做本書的主軸，許多現在「中肯」到不行的字彙都是來自台灣鄉民的創意，讓你邊笑邊學會「脫口而出」好用搞笑的鄉民英文！

英文 netizen 原指花長時間上網的人，鄉民也就是the netizen，在網速極快的台灣，人手一機，大家瘋狂滑手機，現在台灣人人是鄉民啦！「玻璃心」、「空白文」、「這就是人蔘啊」等等現代成語，連當今的新聞和生活的對話中都不停出現，這一些鄉民用語會受到歡迎，因為它們說中台灣人的心吧！它們其實也代表一些台灣特有的現象，例如自由民主的選舉特色，鄉民都被預設為擁有大學學歷但單身的男生，最近在論壇中被大肆討論的文化話題等等，都是非常有趣和值得記錄下來的。感謝兩位作者辛苦地將稿件完成。因為這一些看似簡單有趣的主題和台灣鄉民用語，要跟英語俚語來連結並且將這些流行用語發揮到淋漓盡致，在寫作的過程是很「燒腦」的。希望這本書讓讀者在學英文的過程中，容易與自己熟悉的詞彙連結，幫助讀者在學習英文時有更多的趣味，學到更多在生活中能夠實際使用到的英文俚語和短句。除此之外，本書規劃的對話單元，讓讀者也可以用英文熟練地使用這一些英文慣用語和增加口說能力。希望這一本主題有趣、貼近台灣讀者生活的英文學習書籍可以讓大家在學習英文的道路上，更有趣的學習，有機會看看外國的「鄉民文化」和開口和老外說說這一些「鄉民文化」。

倍斯特編輯部

Contents 目次

PART 01 其實是諧音來的啦！

1. 葉佩雯 010
2. 瘟腥 012
3. 這就是人蔘啊！ 014
4. 無縫接軌 016
5. 加一 018
6. 叫小賀 020
7. 童鞋 022
8. 田僑仔 024
9. 網路酸民、網路小白 026
10. 表特 028
11. 喬 030
12. 踹共 032
13. 放閃 034
14. 空白文 036
15. 銅鋰鋅 038
16. 俗 040
17. 蝦米 042
18. 河蟹 044
19. 婉君 046
20. 肉搜 048
21. 8+9 050
22. BJ4 052

PART
02 你這個人的特質吼！

1. 神人 056
2. 屁孩 058
3. 玻璃心 060
4. 鄉民 062
5. 頗呵 064
6. 媽寶 066
7. 啃老族 068
8. 水水 070
9. 魯蛇 072
10. 丁丁、腦殘 074
11. 小白 076
12. 貓奴 078
13. 中肯 080
14. 太狂了！ 082
15. 海巡署／住海邊 084
16. 爆肝 086
17. 小鮮肉 088
18. 發好人卡 090
19. 自婊 092
20. 冏 094
21. 牛逼、牛 096
22. 給力 098
23. 學霸 100
24. 邊緣人 102

Contents 目次

PART 03 鄉民經典文化！

1. 幻想文 106
2. 帶風向 108
3. 打臉 110
4. 嘴砲 112
5. 推爆 114
6. 裝熟 116
7. 靠譜 118
8. 洋蔥文、加了洋蔥 120
9. 廢文 122
10. 正義魔人 124
11. 撥接魂 126
12. ....系 128
13. 打醬油 130
14. 高富帥 132
15. 白富美 134
16. 神馬 136
17. 搶頭香 138
18. 懶人包 140
19. 幫高調 142

PART 04 網友神回覆！

1. 沒圖沒真相 146
2. 不要問很恐怖！ 148
3. 如何一句話惹惱 150
4. 認真就輸了 152
5. 這是什麼巫術！ 154
6. 不就好棒棒 156
7. 病魔加油 158
8. 噓爆 160
9. 灑花 162
10. 跪求 164
11. 不意外 166
12. 我覺得可以 168
13. 爆雷 170
14. 躺著也中槍 172
15. 也是醉了 174
16. ㄈㄈ尺 176
17. lol 178

PART 05 英文鄉民英語

1. XOXO 182
2. Worth one’s salt 184
3. Conversation blue balls 186
4. Jump the couch 188
5. In a nutshell 190
6. Go nuts 194
7. In the soup 196
8. TBT 198
9. Ootd 200
10. 魔鬼藏在細節裡 202
11. Hashtag 204
12. 佛系 206
13. Smh 208

倍斯特實業坊〉 看版 BESTBOOK

熱門看板	分類看板

PART

01 → 其實是諧音來的啦！

倍斯特實業坊〉看版 BESTBOOK_Unit 1-1 葉佩雯

作者	鄉民英文原來是醬！Internet Slang on PTT
標題	「葉佩雯」Sponsored Content

英文中，「sponsored content」，也就是「廠商贊助的行銷內容」，另一個與這主題相關的概念詞是「content marketing」，指的是發佈有趣且吸引人的文章內容來擴張品牌的能見度。網路上的人氣部落客，時常會分享許多表面上看似純粹分享使用者經驗，但其實是由銷售該產品的廠商主導操作，花錢請知名媒體和部落客為其產品打廣告和刺激銷售的手法。鄉民們使用「葉佩雯」一詞來嘲諷這些手法，當有些新聞和文章推銷某種產品的嫌疑時，回覆中就會出現噓「葉佩雯」，表示鄉民認為文章或新聞不公正是某一家公司的廣告。以逗趣的方式表達，以香港女星的名字「葉佩雯」為「業配文」取其諧音。

MP3 001

In English, "content **marketing**" is called "sponsored content". "Content marketing" means increasing brand and product awareness by posting interesting articles online. It's a form of "content marketing," where the companies pay certain famous **bloggers** or media outlets to **publish** articles sharing their experiences of using products to promote sales. The bloggers try to do so in a way that makes the articles appear less commercialized, but in fact, they are definitely no different than all the other forms of **advertisement.** The netizens use the name of one Hong Kong actress, which is a **homophone** as "content marketing" in Chinese, to tell it is actually an advertisement on the forum.

※發信站：「鄉民這樣說」實業坊(ptt.cc) 來自 140.115.208.44
※文章網址：https://www.ptt.cc/bbs/PttNewhand/M.1452581219.A.FAF.

→ **Johnson123:** Hey! Do you see the article about the amazing wireless vacuum cleaner?

嘿！你有看到那篇有關那台神奇的無線吸塵器文章嗎？

推 **AmyTsai:** Which article?

哪一篇？

→ **Johnson123:** The famous blogger just shares her personal experience of using that piece of machine on the preceding day of Chinese New Year! Her apartment floor in the pictures looks spotless! We should buy one!

那位有名的部落客才剛分享了她在農曆新年大掃除使用那台機器的體驗，她的公寓地板看起來一塵不染！我們也來買一台吧！

推 **AmyTsai:** Dear Johnson, I'm afraid you just fells prey to what's called "sponsored content"!

親愛的強森，恐怕你已經陷入「葉佩雯」的陷阱啦！

單字加油站

單字	詞性	中譯
1. marketing	n.	行銷
2. advertisement	n.	廣告
3. blogger	n.	部落客
4. publish	v.	發佈
5. homophone	n.	同音字

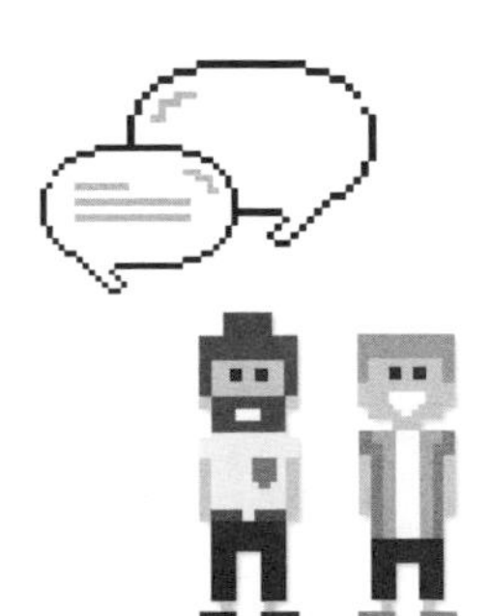

倍斯特實業坊〉看版 BESTBOOK_Unit 1-2 瘟腥

作者	鄉民英文原來是醬！Internet Slang on PTT
標題	瘟腥 That's exactly what the world needs!

「瘟腥」一詞源於「溫馨」，是鄉民表達對於某一件事不滿的一種方式，藉由發音相似、但字體較不雅觀的「瘟腥」，傳達諷刺的概念。例如若鄉民反對某一則新聞報導的立場，即有可能會在留言區回覆「這個新聞實在是好瘟腥喔!」，以反諷的口吻表達自己對這一則新聞的不認同。在英文中，可用「That is exactly what the world needs!」表達類似的情緒，字面上的意思是贊同，背後卻帶有不悅、反諷的立場。

MP3 002

「瘟腥」originates from the word **"warm"** in Chinese to **convey** the **disagreement** of the netizens in a **sarcastic** way. Taiwanese netizens change the original letters into the kuso letters. For instance, if one takes the opposite ground of a piece of the news, he/she may write "How great! XXX is exactly what the world needs!" to **respond to** it. When one does not really appreciate or agree with something, he/she may say "That's exactly what the world needs." By being sarcastic, the words actually reveal a sense of disapproval.

※發信站：「鄉民這樣說」實業坊(ptt.cc) 來自 140.115.208.44

※文章網址：https://www.ptt.cc/bbs/PttNewhand/M.1452581219.A.FAF.

→ **Anna:** Jane, did you know that your favorite celebrity is selling fragrance of her own brand? I think that's pretty cool.

珍，妳知道妳最喜歡的明星推出了自有品牌香水嗎？感覺好酷喔！

推 **Jane:** Really? I can't wait to have it the moment it's on the market! What is the smell going to be like?

真的嗎？真期待，希望它一上市，我就能馬上擁有它！妳知道那是什麼樣的香味嗎？

→ **Tom:** New fragrance? Great! That's exactly what the world needs!

新的香水？太棒了，真的好瘟腥啊！

推 **Anna:** Come on! Don't be so sarcastic! It's fun. I hear the smell is going to be somewhat of a combination of autumn leaves, mint, and dewdrops.

別這麼諷刺嘛！很好玩的，我聽說那香味會是類似楓葉、薄荷及露珠的綜合香味。

→ **Jane:** I will order it online now! There will be a 20% off discount if we pre-order now.

我現在就要在網路上訂購了！現在在她的官網上預購會有八折優惠耶！

單字加油站

單字	詞性	中譯
1. disagreement	n.	不同意
2. sarcastic	adj.	諷刺的
3. respond	v.	回應
4. warm	adj.	溫暖的
5. convey	v.	傳達

倍斯特實業坊〉 看版 BESTBOOK_Unit 1-3 這就是人蔘啊！

作者 鄉民英文原來是醬！Internet Slang on PTT

標題 「這就是人蔘啊！」c’est la vie

鄉民們常在版上分享有關自己親身經歷的悲慘事件及經驗，這時許多網友會在留言區中回覆：「這就是人蔘啊！」，運用諧音的聯想，將中藥材「人蔘」替代原本的詞「人生」，因為中藥材「人蔘」的味道嚐起來很苦，更傳達出了「人生」的本質，在人生中，每個人都將免不了地經歷痛苦和悲傷。在英文中，可以說「c'est la vie」，意思就是「人生就是如此！沒辦法。」，當不如意的事情或糟糕的狀況發生在人生中，而你也無力去改變它的時候，就可以用這一句表達你的無奈，直譯「This is the life.」是完全相反的意思，指的是讚嘆這一刻太棒了，這才是生活啊！

MP3 003

In Taiwan, we see often people share their unpleasant life experiences online. Below we always find people’s comments, and there is one that frequently appears: “It is just a ginseng.” in Chinese. Ginseng, a Chinese herb/traditional medicine, sounds very much like “life” in Chinese. Also, because of its bitterness, having ginseng is like experiencing the hard parts in life, indicating that there’s inevitable harshness in our lives. In English, one may say “C’est la vie.” to convey the same message, and it says that situations of that type happen in life, and you cannot do anything about them. When people say it, it shows how helpless they are and brings self-consolation. However, the literal translation “This is the life.” carries the totally opposite meaning, which means you are very much enjoying the situation you are in and it’s the way life should be.

※發信站：「鄉民這樣說」實業坊(ptt.cc) 來自 140.115.208.44

※文章網址：https://www.ptt.cc/bbs/PttNewhand/M.1452581219.A.FAF.

→ **Suzanne:** Ted, what a coincidence! When are you back in town?

泰德，好巧喔！你什麼時候回來鎮上的？

推 **Ted:** Hello, Suzanne! It's so great running into you like this! I just got back in town yesterday for the **holiday** season.

哈囉，蘇珊！真高興在這裡遇到妳，我昨天才回到鎮上度假。

→ **Suzanne:** Nice! You look great! Are you back with Mary? It's been a while since I last saw you two. You guys are the lovely couple I know!

真棒！你看起來氣色不錯！你跟瑪莉一起回來的嗎？我好久沒見到你倆了，你們可是我所認識最登對的一對情侶！

推 **Ted:** Actually, we **broke up** a few months ago.

其實我們幾個月前分手了。

→ **Suzanne:** Oh! I am so sorry to hear that! How are you holding up?

喔！真抱歉聽到這樣的消息，你還好嗎？

推 **Ted:** Don't be! In fact, I am very **optimistic** about what the future holds now I am back on the market again.

別抱歉！事實上，對於重返約會市場這件事，我還蠻樂觀的。

單字加油站

單字	詞性	中譯
1. holiday	n.	假期
2. break up	v.	分手
3. optimistic	adj.	樂觀的
4. plenty of ...	ph.	許多的
5. complement	v.	互補的

倍斯特實業坊〉看版 BESTBOOK_Unit 1-4 無縫接軌

作者 鄉民英文原來是醬！Internet Slang on PTT

標題

「無縫接軌」No Dry Spell

在網路的世界中，鄉民用語「吳鳳接鬼」取材自成語，「無縫接軌」的音譯轉換，用來指某一對男女朋友在分手之後，其中一方快速開始另一段新的感情，甚至還沒分手前已經與新對象展開曖昧。在鄉民流行用語中，因「無縫」音譯與歷史人物「吳鳳」相同，因此開始以「吳鳳接鬼」這個較有趣的成語來形容一個人的感情狀態。在英文中，會用「There is no dry spell.」來形容某人的感情世界沒有停歇，而「dry spell」也通常暗指性生活，因在情場上順利，也因此沒「無間斷」(no dry spell)。

MP3 004

The online slang 「吳鳳接鬼」 is a convenient **takeover** from a Chinese idiom 「無縫接軌」, indicating that after a couple breaks up, one of them starts a new relationship without **delay**. Even worse is one maybe starts hooking up with someone before they break up. In cyber world, 「無縫」 sounds the same as Taiwanese **historic figure** 「吳鳳」, thus making 「吳鳳接鬼」 a popular and funny way to describe somebody's status of relationship. In English, “there is no dry spell” can deliver the same meaning that one is having a love life non-stop. “Dry spell” could also serve as a pointer regarding someone's sexual life. If one is killing it in love battles, he/she is likely to keep going with “no dry spell”.

※發信站：「鄉民這樣說」實業坊(ptt.cc) 來自 140.115.208.44

※文章網址：https://www.ptt.cc/bbs/PttNewhand/M.1452581219.A.FAF.

→ **Derek:** Hey, do you know that Tom and Kate broke up last month?

嘿，妳知道湯姆跟凱特上個月分手了嗎？

推 **Stella:** Yeah, I just heard about it a few days ago.

嗯，我前幾天有聽說這個消息。

→ **Stella:** Kate is the one who broke it off with Tom. As a matter of fact, I heard there is a mystery guy she's been secretly dating when she's still with Tom.

那你就錯了，她是主動提分手的那一方，而且事實上，我聽說她還沒分手時，就私下偷偷地與一名神秘男子在約會了呢。

推 **Derek:** No way! Are you sure?

真的嗎！妳確定？

→ **Stella:** Positive. As word on the street says, there is no dry spell for Kate as the beauty can practically date whomever she sets her eyes on, right?

非常確定，正如大家所說的，以凱特的姿色，想跟任何她有興趣的男子「吳鳳接鬼」，一定都沒問題的，你說是吧？

單字加油站

單字	詞性	中譯
1. takeover	n.	接手、接管
2. delay	n.	延遲
3. historic	adj.	歷史性的
4. figure	n.	人物

倍斯特實業坊〉看版 BESTBOOK_Unit 1-5 加一

作者 鄉民英文原來是醬！Internet Slang on PTT

標題 加一 Count Me In. / I agree.

「加一」的意思簡單來說就是「我認同」，有時鄉民也會用加號及數字「+1」來代表。假如你認同某一個想法，就可以用「+1」表示。一般而言，「+1」前面會有一個名詞，用來描述所贊同的事物。在英文中可用「same here」這句話來簡單表示「+1」的概念。也可以用「count me in」、「agreed」、「see eye to eye」來表達「對某事有同感，且想參與其中」的概念。

MP3 005

In Taiwan, when you hear people say "plus one", it **basically** means "I agree" or "Count me in". Sometimes netizens even **simplify** it as a plus **symbol** and a number figure as "+1". Whenever you agree with something that is a good, then you say "plus one". **In general**, there is a noun before "plus one", which is the subject that you agree upon. In English, a **similar** expression is "same here". Also, "agreed" and "see eye to eye" deliver a sense of agreement, as well as a will to be part of the whole activity.

※發信站：「鄉民這樣說」實業坊(ptt.cc) 來自 140.115.208.44

※文章網址：https://www.ptt.cc/bbs/PttNewhand/M.1452581219.A.FAF.

→ **Marketing** Supervisor: I propose the theme of the marketing materials should be revolved around our best-selling product, which would be the gluten-free cake with our company's special recipe.

我提議行銷物品的主題應圍繞在我們的暢銷品上，也就是我們那不含麩質的特別食譜蛋糕。

推 **Sales** Manager: I concur. We see eye to eye on this one. On the other hand, have you tried the new cake of our company? I heard the new flavor has huge market potential, but I haven't had the chance to taste it yet.

加一！ 我們意見相同，而另一方面，想問您有試吃過公司上禮拜推出的新蛋糕口味嗎？我聽說新口味蛋糕有很大的市場潛力，但還沒機會試試味道。

→ **Marketing** Manager: Actually, I don't, either. However, I am going to another tasting session for the new cake this afternoon. Would you like to come as well?

事實上，我也還沒有機會嘗試，但我今天下午會去另一場試吃會試試味道，你要一起來嗎？

單字加油站

單字	詞性	中譯
1. basically	adj.	基本上
2. simplify	v.	簡化
3. symbol	n.	符號
4. in general		一般來說
5. similar	adj.	類似的

倍斯特實業坊〉 看版 BESTBOOK_Unit 1-6 叫小賀

作者 鄉民英文原來是醬！Internet Slang on PTT

標題 「叫小賀」 Have the Guts to do Something

「叫小賀」的說法源自於台語，出自台灣本土藝人賀一航分享的搞笑故事。有次他在夜市遇到角頭黑幫，對方問他尊姓大名，而他直白地回答「我叫小賀」。因為「小」在台語中聽起來跟「膽識」相像，而「賀」則跟台語「好」如出一轍。因此「叫小賀」聽起來跟台語「我有膽量」很像 XDD 混混們誤會他的意思，因此在盛怒之下將他毒打一頓。在英文中，可以用「have the guts to do something」來表達類似的意思。

MP3 006

The funning phrase “I’m Xiao-ho” came from the Taiwanese **dialect**. This is a funny story told by the Taiwanese **local** celebrity Ho Chun-Hsiang (賀一航). One time he bumped into some **gangsters** in the night market. They asked him what his name was, and he **frankly** answered “They call me Xiao-ho.” “ They call me Xiao” in Taiwanese dialect sounds very much like the English word “gut”, and “ho” sounds awfully **identic** with “good”. Therefore, “They call me Xiao-ho.” sounds like “I’ve got guts.” in Taiwanese. The gangsters thus mistook his words and thought he was trying to provoke them, so they got irritated, and he was beat up pretty bad. In English, people say “have the guts to do something” meaning he/she dares to do something.

※發信站：「鄉民這樣說」實業坊(ptt.cc) 來自 140.115.208.44
※文章網址：https://www.ptt.cc/bbs/PttNewhand/M.1452581219.A.FAF.

→ **Gretchen:** Hey Josh! Are you ready for the presentation this afternoon?
嗨，喬許！你準備好今天下午的簡報提案了嗎？

推 **Josh:** Hey! I have pulled an all-nighter for this one! I have rehearsed so many times that I feel like I can practically do it in my sleep.
嗨！我昨天為了這個簡報可熬夜準備了一晚！我演練預習了好多次，搞不好我現在連在睡夢中都可以做這份簡報的提案呢！

→ **Gretchen:** Nice! That's so ballsy of you. You really have the guts to do things that many people would find intimidating. After all, the presentation is in front of five hundred people in the audience!
利害！你真勇敢，不愧「叫小賀」，敢做許多人會害怕的任務，畢竟這個簡報提案是在 500 人的觀眾面前進行的。

推 **Josh:** You know what? The trick is not to think about the audience. Just pretend you were talking to yourself. Just imagine that you were only speaking in your bedroom rehearsing.
跟妳說，訣竅在於不要去想下面的觀眾，只要假裝你在跟自己對話，並只要想像你是在自己的房間練習，只是跟自己對話罷了。

單字加油站

單字	詞性	中譯
1. dialect	n.	方言
2. local	adj.	當地的、本土的
3. gangster	n.	流氓、黑道
4. frankly	adv.	直白地
5. identic	adj.	相同的、一樣的

倍斯特實業坊〉 看版 BESTBOOK_Unit 1-7 童鞋

作者 鄉民英文原來是醬！Internet Slang on PTT

標題 「童鞋」fellas、dude、bro、lads

時常聽到的「童鞋」是源自「同學」的台灣國語發音，由於台灣的民眾對於台灣國語的發音感到親切，所以不論是在虛擬的網路世界還是現實生活，台灣人常以這種親切的口吻來稱呼身邊的同伴或好友，拉近彼此的距離。在英文中，可用「fellas (複數)」口語的說法稱呼同伴，稱呼男性的話也可用「dude、bro、lads (複數)」，女性則通常用「girl」，男女通用的字則為「guys (複數)」。

MP3 007

The word 童鞋 (tong-xie, children's shoe) that we usually hear about, is actually a Taiwanese-Chinese **pronunciation** of 同學 (classmate). Since the **unique** Taiwanese-Chinese **tone** makes itself **cordial** for folks in Taiwan, it is broadly used to call upon partners or friends in a sense of **intimacy**, in virtual world and in reality alike. In English, one could use "fellas (plural)" to indicate the same thing. For men, "dude, bro, lads (plural)" could do the same job. For women, "girl". The word "guys (plural)" is rather neutral and can be used for men and women.

※發信站：「鄉民這樣說」實業坊(ptt.cc) 來自 140.115.208.44
※文章網址：https://www.ptt.cc/bbs/PttNewhand/M.1452581219.A.FAF.

→ **Alison111:** Hello, fellas! Welcome to our reading group! For those of you who are here for the first time, please do note that we are here to have fun, to share thoughts, and to have discussions on books.
哈囉，「童鞋」們！歡迎來到我們的讀書會！若你們是第一次參加的話，請記得，我們在這裡的原則是要好玩、享受樂趣，要分享自己的見解。

推 **Lucas121:** That's nice to hear! So essentially the reading group here serves as a platform for us to enjoy the right to freely express our opinions, right? You rock, girl!
聽起來很讚耶！所以這個讀書會的本質，是要提供參與者一個能夠盡情分享自己的想法的舞台，是嗎？妳好棒喔，「童鞋」！

→ **Alison111:** Thank you, bro! That's exactly why I organized this group in the first place, and it'll always be open to anyone who wants to be cerebrally challenged and stimulated through book discussions.
「童鞋」，謝謝你！這正是我當初創立這個讀書會的宗旨，並會繼續歡迎任何有想法、熱衷藉由書籍討論來開發腦力及思考潛力的讀者參與。

單字加油站

單字	詞性	中譯
1. pronunciation	n.	發音
2. tone	n.	語調
3. unique	adj.	獨一無二的
4. cordial	adj.	親切的
5. intimacy	n.	親暱感

倍斯特實業坊〉 看版 BESTBOOK_Unit 1-8 田僑仔

作者 鄉民英文原來是醬！Internet Slang on PTT

標題 「田僑仔」nouveau riche

「田僑仔」是台語發音轉化成國字的用語，口語、書寫皆通用，形容某人在鄉村坐擁大片土地、家財萬貫。這一個詞往往令人聯想到鄉下的田地、三合院等資產，因為擁有大片土地，自然能藉由收租享有豐厚家產，有時候「田僑仔」也有「暴發戶」之意，形容一個人從原本較低的社會階層突然暴富，擠上上流社會。在英文中，坐擁財富，但人文素養欠佳的人，就可以用「nouveau riche」來形容。

MP3 008

「田僑仔」(tian-quao-zai) is a term that originates from Taiwanese but turns directly into **Mandarin** both in **oral** usage and in writing, indicating those who have huge lands and big wealth in countryside. The term also gives out an image of **assets** like farming fields in **countryside** and Sanheyuan. Thanks to their vast property,「田僑仔」are able to gain wealth by renting it out. Base on this reason,「田僑仔」also depicts those who come from lower status, yet become **billionaires** all of a sudden. In English, people who have a whole lot of cash, yet their knowledge and quality don't quite catch up could be described as "nouveau riche".

※發信站：「鄉民這樣說」實業坊(ptt.cc) 來自 140.115.208.44
※文章網址：https://www.ptt.cc/bbs/PttNewhand/M.1452581219.A.FAF.

→ **Annie:** Great to see you, Michael! What brought you back in town?
邁可，真高興見到你！你怎麼會回來老家呀？

推 **Michael:** Hi, how are you? I am back in town to handle some estate dealings. You remember the lands that I inherited from my father? I plan to sell them since I may be moving overseas for good.
哈囉，最近好嗎？我回來處理一些地產的事情，就是有關之前我爸留傳下來的那些土地，我計畫把這些土地賣了，因為我可能打算移民國外了。

→ **Annie:** Really? I think I am definitely going to miss you! As for the lands, it might actually be a good thing to sell them for good, you know, to sever the ties.
真的嗎？我會想念你的！至於那些土地的話，我覺得你把它們賣了或許是件好事，就是把事情切割清楚，你懂的，但我也可瞭解、想像你們田橋仔與家傳土地割捨會有的不捨與難處啊。

單字加油站

單字	詞性	中譯
1. mandarin	n.	普通話
2. oral	adj.	口說的
3. asset	n.	資產
4. countryside	n.	鄉下
5. billionaire	n.	億萬富翁

倍斯特實業坊〉 看版 BESTBOOK_Unit 1-9 酸民

作者 鄉民英文原來是醬！Internet Slang on PTT

標題 網路酸民 Hater 、 網路小白 Internet Troller

「黑特版」是 PTT 論壇上的熱門討論版，「黑特」取自英文「hate」，黑特版則是一個讓鄉民發洩不滿的平台。這個版曾是紅極一時的生活討論版，版上甚至允許公然罵髒話。在英文中，喜歡在網路上對他們不滿的某一件事情、一個人或是一個地方大肆批評，冷嘲熱諷，就被稱為「網路酸民」。網路酸民對他們所見的每一件事都看不順眼。有時網路酸民也指那些看不慣別人成功的人，他們寧願談論他人的缺點，貶低別人。另一個有關的單字是「Internet trolling」(網路小白)，指一群喜歡在網路上刻意發表為了激怒別人的內容的網友，在社群內引起網路論戰，並對這種行為樂此不疲。

MP3 009

「黑特版」is a popular branch-site on Internet forum PTT. 黑特 (hei-te) comes from English word "hate", and「黑特版」(haters' board) is an **outlet** for the netizens to express their negative thoughts. The **platform** was once a go-to **sanctuary** online, which to an extent even allowed people to **curse** openly. In English, those who love to spread their hatred and frustration, things and places on the Internet are called "hater". Haters always disapprove of everything they see. Sometimes haters are those that simply cannot be happy for another person's success. So they would rather be happy they make a point of exposing a flaw in that person and knock other down a notch. Another related word is "Internet troller", indicates someone who likes to post irritated messages and starts quarrels in the online community, and they finds joy in these kinds of peace-shattering behaviors.

※發信站：「鄉民這樣說」實業坊(ptt.cc) 來自 140.115.208.44
※文章網址：https://www.ptt.cc/bbs/PttNewhand/M.1452581219.A.FAF.

→ **Wendy:** Hey, Linda! What's wrong? Why you look so upset?
哈囉，琳達！怎麼啦？怎麼看起來臉色不太好？

推 **Linda:** Hello, Wendy. Thanks for asking, but I'm so riled up right now. You know I have a blog, right? I just posted some of my personal thoughts on politics last night, and only to wake up to some mean, hateful comments from Internet troll.
哈囉，溫蒂，謝謝您的關心，但我現在很生氣，妳知道我有在經營一個部落格，是吧？我昨晚發文分享我個人對於政治的一些看法，但沒想到今早一起來，竟發現一些網路小白在底下留了難聽、充滿敵意的留言。

→ **Wendy:** Oh no! It sounds like what you're up against the omnipresent Internet trolls who are literally too many to fight! Just pay them no mind and keep voicing your opinions on the blog!
喔不！聽起來你似乎在與無處不在的網路小白抗衡，但這種人實在太多了！不要理他們，繼續在妳的部落格發表妳的意見吧！

推 **Linda:** You know what? I will! I won't let some mean-spirited behaviors of Internet trolling stop me from having a voice. Thanks, Wendy!
妳知道嗎？我會的！我不會讓這些立意不善的網路「黑特」行為妨礙我發表我想說的言論，謝啦，溫蒂！

單字加油站

單字	詞性	中譯
1. platform	n.	平台
2. outlet	n.	發洩方式
3. sanctuary	n.	聖地
4. curse	v.	罵粗話

倍斯特實業坊〉 看版 BESTBOOK_Unit 1-10 表特

作者 鄉民英文原來是醬！Internet Slang on PTT

標題 「表特」Beauty

「表特」這一個詞起源於鄉民在 PTT 成立了名為「表特版」的討論區，「表特」是英文「beauty」的音譯。看網路看版名就可以推測，此版的目的是為了討論有亮麗外表的帥哥美女，且網友會在這一個版張貼型男正妹的圖片讓網友欣賞、點評，所以這一個版大受歡迎，擁有高人氣。英文與此相關的用語有「情人眼裡出西施」“Beauty is in the eye of the beholder.”，以及經典名句「美麗是膚淺的」“Beauty is only skin-deep”，可見對美的觀念古今中外皆然，但太過美麗出眾的人物，往往都是可遠觀不可褻玩焉啊！

MP3 010

The term「表特」(biao-te) comes along after netizens established a platform in online forum PTT, which was called 「表特版」(biao-te board).「表特」is borrowed from English word “beauty”, and just from the name itself. One can tell it is a platform talking about beautiful girls and hot guys. Also, members post photos of hot dudes and cute girls for viewers to **rate**, and the platform is **nicknamed** “**charming** dudes ‘n chicks”. In English, **relevant** expressions include “Beauty is in the eye of the beholder.” and the **classic** old one “Beauty is only skin-deep.” No matter where and the time in the world, people appreciate beautiful things. But such godly figures are usually unreachable for ordinary people.

※發信站：「鄉民這樣說」實業坊(ptt.cc) 來自 140.115.208.44
※文章網址：https://www.ptt.cc/bbs/PttNewhand/M.1452581219.A.FAF.

→ **Andy:** Hey, man! What's up? I saw your new girlfriend on Facebook. She's gorgeous, you lucky man!

哈囉，兄弟！近來可好？我在臉書上看到你的新女友，她很正耶，你實在太幸運了！

推 **Alex:** Thanks, man! I'm telling you! However, some of my family members seem to think otherwise.

謝啦，兄弟！她是我這一生見過最美麗的女人，真的！但是我的某些家人似乎不這麼覺得。

→ **Andy:** What do you mean? It's fine. Just don't let them get in the way of your happiness. Besides, haven't you ever heard of the saying "beauty is in the eye of the beholder"? It's you who're going to spend the rest of your life with the woman you love, not them!

怎麼說？沒關係，不要讓他們阻礙你追尋快樂，並且，你聽過諺語「情人眼裡出西施」吧？是你要跟你所愛的女人終生相許一輩子，而不是他們！

推 **Alex:** I think you're totally right! Besides, beauty is only skin-deep, right? My girlfriend has the most amazing personality ever!

你是對的！美貌只是膚淺的、一時的，是吧？我的女朋友有著最迷人的性格！

單字加油站

單字	詞性	中譯
1. rate	v.	評分
2. nickname	v.	幫…取綽號
3. charming	adj.	有魅力的
4. relevant	adj.	相關的
5. classic	adj.	經典的

倍斯特實業坊〉 看版 BESTBOOK_Unit 1-11 喬

作者	鄉民英文原來是醬！Internet Slang on PTT
標題	「喬」Coordinate

「喬」這個字來自台語的音譯，因為台灣某一任立法院院長，能在黑白兩道居中斡旋，因此獲封「喬王」美稱。簡單來說，「喬」指的是協助不同立場的兩方「協調並達成共識」的意思，甚至是完全相反的兩方。在英文中，用「coordinate」這個動詞表達類似含義，另有一個趣味的諺語「揮揮魔法杖」，意指不需耗費太多力氣、資源，就能輕鬆把事情「喬」、處理好，如同有魔杖一般，揮一揮就讓事情塵埃落定。

MP3 011

The term 喬 (quao) comes from Taiwanese pronunciation. There was once a **minister** of Legislative Yuan of Taiwan, who, during his tenure of office, was **awarded** "喬王" in praise of his **capability** of dancing between the police and the gang. 喬, in short, means to **negotiate** and make deal between the two different parties, even opposite. In English, one can simply use the verb "coordinate" to express the same thing. There is also an interesting **idiom**, wave a magic wand, indicating settling things without many troubles or resources. Just like a magic wand, you wave it and it's all done.

※發信站：「鄉民這樣說」實業坊(ptt.cc) 來自 140.115.208.44
※文章網址：https://www.ptt.cc/bbs/PttNewhand/M.1452581219.A.FAF.

→ **Teresa:** So for the event next week, we've still got so many items to cross off on our to-do list! Let me see, there's food & beverage to take care of, and there's the entertainment aspect….

有關下個星期的活動，我們還有好多待辦事項須處理，我看看，有食物與茶水需要處理，還有娛樂的部份…

推 **Megan:** Relax! We're going to be fine, and the event is going to run smoothly! After all, we've just hire the event coordinator Rita, whose reputation certainly precedes her in the event industry.

放輕鬆啦！一切都會安好，且活動會進行得很順利的！畢竟，我們已經聘僱了活動專案執行莉塔，她在活動籌劃業界的名聲可是非常好的。

→ **Teresa:** Yeah, I heard she can clean up any mess and turn up a fabulous event in no time. I certainly hope she can swoop in here and just waves her magic wand, and we both can take some time to breathe and relax.

嗯，我聽說她能夠解決任何一團亂的東西，並即時、快速地舉辦一場完美的活動，我真希望她能夠趕快來報到，然後稍微揮揮她的魔杖把事情都「喬」好，然後我倆就可稍微呼吸、放鬆一下了。

單字加油站

單字	詞性	中譯
1. minister	n.	部長
2. award	v.	獲頒…
3. capability	n.	能力
4. negotiate	v.	協商
5. idiom	n.	慣用語、成語

倍斯特實業坊〉 看版 BESTBOOK_Unit 1-12 踹共

作者 鄉民英文原來是醬！Internet Slang on PTT

標題 「踹共」face off

鄉民用語「踹共」來自台語發音，是要人「出來面對、講清楚」的意思，帶有一絲挑釁的意味。因為來源饒富興味，在媒體及報章雜誌廣泛地運用之下，現在已經成為台灣人耳熟能詳的網路用語。因為他很簡單好用，在英文中，可以用「face off」或「clear the air」表達相同概念，都傳達要人當面把事情講清楚的意思。「face the music」則指一個人勇敢面對事情的真相。

MP3 012

The term「踹共」(chuai-gong) comes from a Taiwanese word. It is rather a fun way to tell people to come out, explain something and carry with a sense of provocation. Thanks to its **intriguing origin**, it was wildly used on TV **media** as well on magazines and newspapers. **Nowadays**, it is without doubt one of the most heard-of Internet slangs in Taiwan society because it is simple and easy to use. In English, “face off” or “clear the air” bear the similar meanings, both demanding the subject party to come out in person and explain in **detail**. “Face the music”, however, means that someone ultimately is brave enough to face the truth.

※發信站：「鄉民這樣說」實業坊(ptt.cc) 來自 140.115.208.44

※文章網址：https://www.ptt.cc/bbs/PttNewhand/M.1452581219.A.FAF.

→ **Kathy0710:** Hey, did you hear about the disagreement between Henry and Judy. I heard it's quite an explosive argument! Do you know what it is about?

嘿，你有聽說亨利跟茱蒂之間的不合嗎？聽說是個蠻火爆的場面耶！你知道不合的原因是什麼嗎？

推 **Albert_aa:** I heard about it, but I only know that there has been stuff brewing between the two of them quite some time, and it seemed that they just could not contain the resentment towards each other anymore and finally face off!

我有聽說，但我只知道他們已經不合一段時間了，但他們似乎已無法控制對對方不滿的情緒，而終於出來「踹共」了！

→ **Kathy0710:** I wished they'd had cleared the air in a calmer and more mature manner.

我希望他們是以較冷靜、成熟的方式「踹共」。

單字加油站

單字	詞性	中譯
1. intriguing	adj.	令人玩味的
2. origin	n.	起源
3. media	n.	媒體
4. nowadays	adv.	現今
5. detail	n.	細節

倍斯特實業坊〉看版 BESTBOOK_Unit 1-13 放閃

作者 鄉民英文原來是醬！Internet Slang on PTT

標題 「放閃」Blinding Light

台灣人將情侶在公開場合擁抱、接吻、對對方表達愛意的動作，或是情侶將充滿愛意的互動發布在網路上，這個行為被稱作「放閃」。台灣網友喜歡稱戀愛中的情侶「閃光」，因為這些人常常愛得過火，周遭的事物都視而不見，只顧著大秀恩愛，在單身的人眼裡特別刺眼，就像是閃光一樣。現在在台灣「閃光」一詞可當作名詞代指伴侶，也可當作形容詞，但這個字往往帶有一絲羨慕、嫉妒又惱怒。如果一對情侶表現得太超過，讓人「不忍卒睹」，就可以叫他們「去開房間」(get a room)。有時候對單身狗而言，秀恩愛真有點讓人難以忍受，就像閃光一樣刺眼。

MP3 013

When the couples hug, kiss or express their love to each other in a public setting, or the couples post their sweet moments on the social media, which we call it 「放閃」 in Taiwan. Taiwanese netizens like to describe those who are so in love as "the blinding light「閃光」", in the eyes of single people because these people are usually too in love that they **ignore** their **surroundings** and just show off their affection. Their public display of affection is like a blinding light to those who are single. The word 「閃光」 not only can be used as a noun to indicate the couple, but also can be used as an adjective, which can convey a sense of appreciation, **annoyance** or **jealousy**. 「閃光」 more or less equals to the **phenomenon** of PDA, public display of affection. If the couple behaves way too much for others to bear, one may say "get a room!" Sometimes, those sweet moments between couples are just unbearable for those who aren't quite in love and are single, just like extremely bright and making it difficult for people to see.

※發信站：「鄉民這樣說」實業坊(ptt.cc) 來自 140.115.208.44
※文章網址：https://www.ptt.cc/bbs/PttNewhand/M.1452581219.A.FAF.

→ **Jacky1212:** Look that those two love birds over there on the bench!

你看那板凳上的那對情侶！

推 **Supersmith:** Oh! Do they really need to be that passionate about each other? People are getting way too comfortable with public display of affection (PDA).

喔！他們有必要這麼熱情嗎？現代人真的太開放，越來越「閃光」了耶。

→ **Jacky1212:** That's something to be mindful of when you are visiting certain countries with the conservative culture since you would not wish to offend anyone.

如果你到文化比較保守的國家旅遊時就要注意這種事情，這樣才不會冒犯到他們。

推 **Supersmith:** That's true, and I'd always have to constrain myself from yelling "Get a room!" to couples who're really being too comfortable with their public display of affection.

真的，而我每次都要克制自己對大曬恩愛、「閃光」的情侶怒吼「別再放閃了！」。

單字加油站

單字	詞性	中譯
1. ignore	v.	無視、忽略
2. surroundings	n.	周遭環境
3. annoyance	n.	惱怒
4. jealousy	n.	嫉妒
5. phenomenon	n.	現象

倍斯特實業坊〉 看版 BESTBOOK_Unit 1-14 空白文

作者	鄉民英文原來是醬！Internet Slang on PTT
標題	空白文 PDA on the Internet

除了「閃光」、「墨鏡」及「可魯」之外，鄉民也常說「空白文」，其緣由也出自跟上一篇一樣的邏輯，因為某一個人發布的文章太過令人羨慕，或是太過於曬恩愛或是太過令人羨慕，而大放「閃光」、令人幾近看不到眼前的事物，只看的到一片空白，因此稱為「空白文」。在英文中，「Public display of affection」縮寫(PDA)指的是情侶在公眾場合秀出親密舉動，就是中文的「曬恩愛」。空白文就是在網路上曬恩愛啦！另外一個英文字「lovebirds」形容一對深愛對方、喜歡在別人面前曬恩愛的情侶，其緣由來自一種名為「lovebird」的鸚鵡，這種鸚鵡跟伴侶非常地恩愛，也因此被用來形容喜歡在公眾場合秀恩愛的情侶。

MP3 014

Apart from “the blinding light”, “sunglasses” and 可魯 (ke-lu), Taiwanese netizens also like to use「空白文」“blank context” to call this kind of posts since if a post demonstrates too many details of couples that make others jealous, or the affection within context is way too **obvious**, then “the blinding light” is just too bright that other people can’t even see a thing. In English, the phrase “Public display of affection” (PDA) means the couples’ acts of physical intimacy in public. The Chinese slang 「空白文」 is “PDA on the Internet”. Another word “lovebirds” refers to a couple that tends to show their affection in public. The expression comes from a kind of parrot called lovebird. This kind of parrot would always show **extremely** care for its **partner**. Thus, the spirit is passed down to portray couples that are not afraid of showing their heart in public.

※發信站：「鄉民這樣說」實業坊(ptt.cc) 來自 140.115.208.44
※文章網址：https://www.ptt.cc/bbs/PttNewhand/M.1452581219.A.FAF.

→ **Josh:** I am so desperate! I just can't seem to find true love! Everywhere I turn, I am surrounded by lovebirds. They are always all over each other, with no problem of public display of affection towards each other at all. Why everyone seems to find the right one with such ease, but me!

我感到好絕望啊！我總是找不到真愛！但我身邊總是充滿了 po「空白文」的情侶們，他們總是在公眾場合擁吻，一點都不會為他們「放閃」的行為而感到不好意思耶，為什麼大家似乎都能夠輕而易舉地找到真愛，但我卻無法呢！

推 **Nick:** Calm down, man! It doesn't help when you feel desperate about the situation. You need a dating coach to put you through your paces. You know, to up your game a little.

你需要冷靜一下！你這樣感到絕望，並不會讓情況更好，你需要一個約會老師來開導你，你懂得，讓他來讓你更有魅力。

單字加油站

單字	詞性	中譯
1. apart from	除了…之外	
2. logical	adj.	有邏輯性的
3. obvious	adj.	明顯的
4. extremely	adv.	極度地
5. partner	n.	伴侶、夥伴

倍斯特實業坊〉 看版 BESTBOOK_Unit 1-15 銅鋰鋅

作者	鄉民英文原來是醬！Internet Slang on PTT
標題	「銅鋰鋅」Hyper-empathy、Empathy

網路用語「銅鋰鋅」，其來源即是「同理心」一詞的諧音，其出處是來自台灣 2015 年暑假發生的八仙樂園塵爆事件，在網路論壇上出現大量有關傷者的討論，另一些鄉民會以「沒同理心」和「要有同理心」回應，因為這一個字被過度提起，所以鄉民以化學元素的諧音字「銅鋰鋅」轉化原本的意思和字形，衍生出帶有集體盲目和濫情的負面意涵。若要完整表達「銅鋰鋅」的「濫情」意味，在英文中，心理學的字詞「hyper- empathy」可以形容過度的同情心和憐憫。

MP3 015

The term 銅鋰鋅 (tong-li-xin, copper, lithium and zinc) comes from「同理心」(empathy). It's a play on the similar sound of the two. The term became popular after the New Taipei water park **explosion** in 2015. Back then, the cyber forum was flooded with discussions about the **injured**. In response to some of the topics, people always left comments like "you have no empathy" or "Try have some empathy!". The word empathy (同理心) thus became kind of a **cliché**. That's why after a while, people started to use chemical elements 銅鋰鋅 to replace it. By deforming both the form and the meaning, it transmits a sense of collective blindness and empathy **abuse**. To fully convey the sarcasm behind「銅鋰鋅」, **psychological** term "hyper-empathy" may be the go-to word, which indicates one's indulgence on empathy and pity.

※發信站：「鄉民這樣說」實業坊(ptt.cc) 來自 140.115.208.44
※文章網址：https://www.ptt.cc/bbs/PttNewhand/M.1452581219.A.FAF.

→ **Steven663:** Hey, did you see the news about the celebrity getting a divorce? Who'd know that their marriage is in trouble? They seem to be such a perfect couple on the surface.

嘿，你有看到有關那個影星準備離婚的新聞嗎？誰會知道他們的婚姻遇到瓶頸呀！他們乍看之下還真是完美的一對伴侶啊。

推 **Fiona525:** That's really shocking. I feel very bad for them. Am I being hyper-empathetic? I didn't sleep well last night because of this news.

真的很令人震驚，真為他們感到難過，不知是否是我太有「銅鋰鋅」了，因為這則新聞，讓我昨晚難過到睡不著覺。

→ **Steven:** That's a bit melodramatic. The news is definitely not a joyful event, but not insomnia for that! You're such a sympathizer.

這就有點誇張了，這則新聞當然不是件好事，但別為了這件事而失眠啊！你真是太有「銅鋰鋅」了。

單字加油站

單字	詞性	中譯
1. explosion	n.	爆炸
2. injured	n.	受傷的人
3. cliché	n.	陳腔濫調
4. abuse	n.	濫用
5. psychological	adj.	心理學的

倍斯特實業坊〉看版 BESTBOOK_Unit 1-16 俗	
作者	鄉民英文原來是醬！Internet Slang on PTT
標題	「俗」vulgar

「俗」這個用字來自台語，是指某人的行為、裝扮和舉止很過時，未見過世面或是沒有接受良好教育的樣子；在英文中，有許多的字眼可用來形容「俗」的意思，如用「hillbilly」和「redneck」(鄉巴佬)等單字，也可用「unsophisticated」、「unrefined」來表示「俗」的意思，或是「vulgar」、「tacky」等形容詞也都可用來形容某人的行為舉止粗「俗」、沒有教養。

MP3 016

「俗」this word originates from Taiwanese to describe someone's behaviors or clothes are out-of-date, like going out in the world for the first time or not very well educated. In English, there are many words to describe this kind of person, such as, hillbilly, redneck, unsophisticated and unrefined. The word "vulgar" and "tacky" are the adjective to explain one's behaviors are rude, unpleasant and without manners.

※發信站：「鄉民這樣說」實業坊(ptt.cc) 來自 140.115.208.44
※文章網址：https://www.ptt.cc/bbs/PttNewhand/M.1452581219.A.FAF.

→ **Greta:** Hey, did you attend your cousin's wedding? It's just one month ago, right?

嘿，你有參加你表弟的婚禮嗎？一個月前，對吧？

推 **Frank:** I did. It's such a shame that you couldn't make it.

我有，妳沒來真是可惜呀。

→ **Greta:** I know, but I got stuck in a lay-over as the flight got canceled. I was really upset about it.

對呀，但我要轉機的班機臨時被取消了，當下真的很生氣。

推 **Frank:** Let me tell you, the wedding itself is really elegant and sweet. However, it all turns sour when some of the attendees had too much to drink. Those rednecks really display some vulgar and tacky behaviors while being inebriated, and almost ruined the whole wedding!

婚禮本身真的很高雅、甜蜜，但後來有些賓客喝多了，把場面搞砸，當那些粗「俗」的人喝醉時，他們的行為舉止好「俗」喔，還差點把整個婚禮搞砸了！

→ **Greta:** Oh my, I'm glad I miss that.

天啊，真高興沒有親眼目睹那些戲碼。

單字加油站

單字	詞性	中譯
1. elegant	adj.	優雅的
2. attendee	n.	參加者
3. vulgar	adj.	粗俗的
4. behavior	n.	行為
5. out-of-date	adj.	過時的

倍斯特實業坊〉 看版 BESTBOOK_Unit 1-17 蝦米

作者	鄉民英文原來是醬！Internet Slang on PTT
標題	「蝦米」I beg your pardon? What?

這個流行用語「蝦米」是源自台語「什麼」的音譯，台語中的「蝦米」和國語的「什麼」發音很接近，這個用法顯得有趣又搞笑，漸漸在台灣的網路和媒體上變得流行。當你沒聽清楚對方所說的話，禮貌地請對方再講一次時，英文可用「I beg your pardon?」，直接簡單地用「Sorry?」、「Excuse me?」。另一個用法是表示驚訝，不敢相信自己聽到什麼，英文可用「What?」。這個字的真正意思是一種食材「蝦米」，則是用單字「dried sea shrimp」，乾燥的蝦米是常見中式食材的一種，另一個單字「prawn」雖然也是「蝦子」的意思，但是用來指體型較大的種類。

MP3 017

This Taiwanese slang word 「蝦米」 originates from Taiwanese “What?”, and these two pronunciations are alike and using 「蝦米」 seems funny and silly. It becomes a popular term in media and online in Taiwan now. In English, if you don’t hear people, then you politely ask “I beg your pardon?” to ask them to say it again. “Sorry?”, “Excuse me?” are less formal ways of saying this. It is also used to show your surprise. When people cannot believe what they hear, they say “What?” in questions that show they’re surprised or don’t believe. The real meaning of「蝦米」is one kind of common Asian food ingredients, and in English is called “dried sea shrimp.” Another word “prawn” is another kind of bigger shrimps.

※發信站：「鄉民這樣說」實業坊(ptt.cc) 來自 140.115.208.44
※文章網址：https://www.ptt.cc/bbs/PttNewhand/M.1452581219.A.FAF.

推 **Stephen1212:** Hey, you know what I'm actually going to a seafood restaurant to meet some of my buddies. Would you join us to have some tantalizing grilled shrimps?

嘿，我其實跟幾個好兄弟約好要去海鮮餐廳吃晚餐，妳想加入我們嗎？有很美味的烤「蝦米」喔！

→ **Stella_55:** Sure, the offer is too tempting to pass. I'll just drop my bags home and meet you guys there.

好！聽起來太誘人了，我會先回家放包包，再去餐廳找你們好了。

推 **Stephen1212:** Not a problem! The restaurant is at the intersection of 8th avenue and 17th street. I think it's just a few blocks from where you live.

好！餐廳是在第八大道跟 17 街的交叉口，好像離妳家只有幾個街區距離。

→ **Stella_55:** I beg your pardon? I'm actually not good with direction.

「蝦米」？我其實很沒方向感耶。

→ **Stella_55:** Okay, I know where it is now!

好的，我這樣知道在哪裡了！

單字加油站

單字	詞性	中譯
1. coincidence	n.	巧合，碰巧的事
2. politely	adv.	有禮貌地
3. surprised	adj.	驚訝的
4. ingredient	n.	材料
5. slang	n.	俚語

倍斯特實業坊〉看版 BESTBOOK_Unit 1-18 河蟹

作者　鄉民英文原來是醬！Internet Slang on PTT

標題　「河蟹」Rule with An Iron Fist

網路用語「河蟹」是取「和諧」一詞的諧音，因為兩者發音相像，便用這個詞來代稱中國敏感的政治環境。這個詞來自中國網路世界，因為中國推行「和諧社會政策」，政府有權利控管並封鎖網路上各種對政府不利的新聞及言論。河蟹既然是一種螃蟹，網友便取其意象，諷刺政府專制的作風就跟螃蟹橫著走路一樣霸道無禮。這種反諷的意味也可用英文片語「rule with an iron fist」表示，意思是用無可匹敵的鐵腕手段治國。

MP3 018

Cyber term 河蟹 (river crab) is a take from 和諧 harmony. Since the two sounds alike, it is used to avoid the political **sensitive** situation in Mainland China. The term can be seen online in China region. Due to the Harmonious Society program of Chinese Communist Party, Chinese government has the power to control and **block** news to a web post on the Internet that has **negative** impact on them. 河蟹, which is a kind of crab, thus jumps into play as an outlet for such "**forbidden** thoughts". Also, people use this term to make fun of the authority because their dictatorship is as awkward as a crab walking sideways. Its irony could be compared with the term "rule with an iron fist", which literally means to rule with an unbeatable power.

※發信站：「鄉民這樣說」實業坊(ptt.cc) 來自 140.115.208.44
※文章網址：https://www.ptt.cc/bbs/PttNewhand/M.1452581219.A.FAF.

→ **Tommy:** Hello! How's your life now while you're working in China?
哈囉！在大陸的工作生活如何呀？

推 **Evelyn:** Hey, it's pretty good. I am adjusting pretty well to its culture and lifestyle in China, but the only thing that I am still not used to is the way I surf on the Internet.
嘿，還不錯，對於大陸的文化及生活方式適應的還不錯，但唯一不習慣的是上網的方式。

→ **Tommy:** Oh yes, I know that the China government rules with an iron fist when it comes to the freedom of speech on the Internet, especially any kind of negative comments on the government.
喔，是的，我知道大陸政府對於網路上言論自由的「河蟹」作風，尤其是任何有關他們的負面評論。

推 **Evelyn:** That's correct. Despite the fact that there are many great Chinese alternative websites, like Google and Facebook, and it's stills not the same as the information you get online is much controlled and tailored in favor of the government!
沒錯，所以儘管有很多大陸版的網站類似谷哥或是臉書，但還是不一樣，因為你得到的資訊多是受過審查的，且大多是有益於政府的資訊。

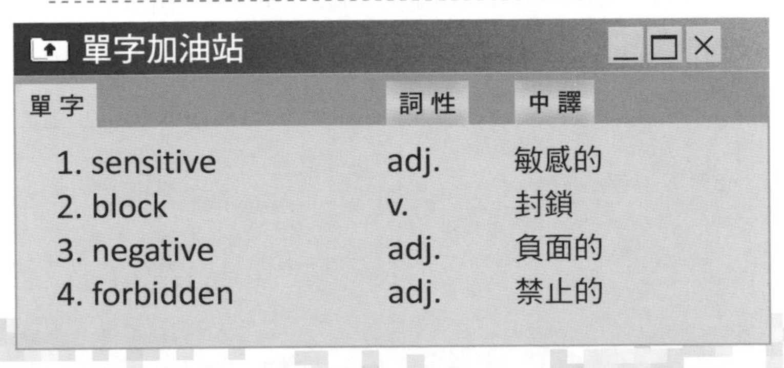

單字加油站

單字	詞性	中譯
1. sensitive	adj.	敏感的
2. block	v.	封鎖
3. negative	adj.	負面的
4. forbidden	adj.	禁止的

倍斯特實業坊〉 看版 BESTBOOK_Unit 1-19 婉君

作者 鄉民英文原來是醬！Internet Slang on PTT

標題 「婉君」Media manipulation

網路用語「婉君」一詞指的就是「網路軍團」的意思，因「婉君」跟「網軍」發音很像而拿來當代稱。這一個詞取自台灣 1990 年代的當紅電視劇名《婉君》，指某一些特定政治背景的網友們喬裝成一般網路使用者，組成有系統的「網路軍團」，並在網路上發表對支持政黨、團體或組織有利的言論，試圖操作輿論，英文片語「media manipulation」指的是利用媒體對大眾持續灌輸某個政黨或團體刻意編造的印象，讓社會大眾不知不覺的接受，達到政黨和團體的利益。

MP3 019

Internet **keyword** 婉君 (wan-jun) actually means 網路軍團 (internet army). Thanks to the awfully identic **pronunciation**, 婉君 is now a slang for the infamous Internet army itself. The term is taken from a popular TV show in the 90s. It refers to a group of netizens with certain political background who **disguise** themselves as general Internet users. What they aim to do is to actually form a **systematic** "army" and post comments online that favors their supporting party, group or organization. The reason why they operate in such is to manipulate public opinions. The term "media **manipulation**" indicates that someone benefits from the media by using it to build up certain image of a party or group, thus creep their ideas in people and ultimately achieve predestined goals for their groups.

※發信站：「鄉民這樣說」實業坊(ptt.cc) 來自 140.115.208.44
※文章網址：https://www.ptt.cc/bbs/PttNewhand/M.1452581219.A.FAF.

→ **Sharonlin:** Hey, what do you think about the coming election?
嘿，你對於即將到來的大選有何看法呢？

推 **Ted0555:** I'm not sure at the moment. Every day I read the latest news on the Internet, but sometimes the comments below are so polarized that I don't know which side to put my trust in.
我還不確定耶，我每天都有在網路上追蹤最新的消息，但有時候新聞下面的意見區塊，總是有許多兩極的評論，所以我還不確定要信任哪一派啊！

→ **Sharonlin:** I know! The netizens of politics today are certainly not shy when it comes to swaying the public to their favored parties on the Internet. But some of their comments seem to cross the line.
對呀！今日的政治「婉君」們可是一點都不害羞，很積極地在網路上試圖影響大眾支持他們所支持的黨派，但有時候他們的評論太超過了。

推 **Ted0555:** Totally! It's good to state your point of view in a rational manner, but when it's about blindly bashing the other candidates? Not so good, I'm afraid.
真的！若你能夠理性地闡述你的觀點是一件很好的事，但若只是盲目地毀謗其它候選人，實在是不好的呀！

單字加油站

單字	詞性	中譯
1. keyword	n.	關鍵字
2. pronunciation	n.	發音
3. disguise	v.	偽裝
4. systematic	adj.	有系統的
5. manipulation	n.	操弄

倍斯特實業坊〉 看版 BESTBOOK_Unit 1-20 肉搜

作者	鄉民英文原來是醬！Internet Slang on PTT
標題	肉搜 Cyber manhunt

在這個資訊爆炸的時代，最好別以為還能為善不欲人知─或是做壞事沒人知道。政府的監視系統是一回事，人手一機的拍照功能的影響力更是無遠弗屆。沒扶老人過馬路？騎車撞了人就跑？通常「兇手」很快就會被肉搜出來。肉搜通常是透過網路媒介，例如有個人資料的社群媒體等，揪出某一個特定人物的行為，透過強大的鄉民，「匪徒」往往沒三兩下就被肉搜出來。肉搜也很常用在尋找正妹帥哥上，想認識捷運上的美女嗎？說不定可以請網友肉搜喔！

MP3 020

In this information **explosive** age, there's no way that one can do good deeds without being noticed—or worse, commit crime and be off the hook. Authority **surveillance** system is one thing; mobile devices held in each and every one of us are more powerful: with its camera, they are just **omnipresent**. Letting **senior citizens** crossing the street alone? Hit and run with a scooter? The "suspect" is usually being located by cyber manhunt. Cyber manhunt is the action of finding certain personnel through Internet media, usually social media that have personal information. With the help of the vast netizens, the "**murderer**" would be captured with a blink of an eye. Also, quite often HFSE is used for looking up hot dudes or chicks. If you want to know who the hot girl is on MRT, asking for cyber manhunt may be an option.

※發信站：「鄉民這樣說」實業坊(ptt.cc) 來自 140.115.208.44
※文章網址：https://www.ptt.cc/bbs/PttNewhand/M.1452581219.A.FAF.

→ **Ryan:** You know the guy that ate in an all-you-can-eat buffet for free? Turns out he is a millionaire!

雷恩：妳知道那個在吃到飽餐廳吃霸王餐的傢伙嗎？想不到他竟是個百萬富翁！

推 **Judy:** I know! Isn't him the guy that was on the news earlier?

茱蒂：我知道！是不是剛剛新聞在播的那個人？

→ **Ryan:** The restaurant posted his photo online and boom! Two days later, people cyber man-hunted him and bust him out!

雷恩：餐廳把他的照片上傳網路，兩天後，網友就把他肉搜出來了！

推 **Judy:** Why would he do that? He is so rich!

茱蒂：他怎麼這麼沒品？明明很有錢！

→ **Ryan:** Maybe that's what makes him rich, by eating everywhere for free.

雷恩：也許這就是他有錢的原因吧，到處吃霸王餐。

單字加油站

單字	詞性	中譯
1. explosive	adj.	爆炸的
2. surveillance	n.	監視
3. omnipresent	adj.	無所不在的
4. senior	citizen	老年人（的含蓄說法）
5. murderer	n.	殺人犯

倍斯特實業坊〉 看版 BESTBOOK_Unit 1-21 8+9

作者	鄉民英文原來是醬！Internet Slang on PTT
標題	「8+9」Thugs

「8+9」是台灣廟會團體中八家將的諧音，是 PTT 內的流行鄉民用語，帶有貶意。因為台灣部分的八家將組織與黑幫有連結，所以參加宮廟活動的年輕人常見是一些逞兇鬥狠的青少年，現在較多是指一群年輕失學的青少年或是愛逞兇鬥狠的小流氓。這一個詞開始流行是因為在鄉民眼中，比起擁有大學學歷的宅男魯蛇們，這些痞痞的「8+9」好像都交到了正妹女朋友，這一點讓鄉民們吃味也感到不滿，開始在 PTT 掀起相關的討論。在英文中，較常用「thug」來指街頭小混混，跟「gangster」有不一樣的意思，這兩個單字的意思偏向罪犯或是黑幫幫派成員。

MP3 021

In Mandarin, “8+9”sounds like the group Ba Jia Jiang (八家將) of Chinese folk **beliefs**. However, when it comes to Taiwanese netizens, it becomes a negative term. In fact, the **organization** of Ba Jia Jiang in Taiwan is more or less related to the gangsters, and people taking part in Ba Jia Jiang are often rogues. The term “8+9” now refers to thug that drop out of school or those who like to stir up a fight because it is a homophone of Ba Jia Jiang. The reason why this term went viral is because comparing to these single college **graduates** “otakus” or “losers”, these naughty “8+9” seem to have hot chicks as girlfriends. Some netizens simply could not **tolerate** that, thus started such discussions online. In English, “thug” refers to a little rogue, kind of different from the gangsters which tend to be criminals or mafia members.

※發信站：「鄉民這樣說」實業坊(ptt.cc) 來自 140.115.208.44
※文章網址：https://www.ptt.cc/bbs/PttNewhand/M.1452581219.A.FAF.

→ **Judy:** I can't bear seeing anymore words from these thugs.

茱蒂：我再也受不了這些 8+9 的發言了。

推 **Ryan:** I know, right? I mean who do they think they are?

雷恩：我懂，對吧？我的意思是，他們以為自己是誰啊？

→ **Judy:** Check this out: if wolf turns back, either is to return the favor, or to revenge.

茱蒂：看看這一句：狼若回頭，不是報恩，就是報仇。

推 **Ryan:** Christ, and it is probably from a 15-year-old.

雷恩：老天，而且打這句話的人可能只是個 15 歲少年。

→ **Judy:** Yeah. What do they know about revenge? Do they even live long enough to revenge on anything?

茱蒂：對啊，他們懂什麼報仇？他們有老到需要跟別人報什麼仇嗎？

單字加油站

單字	詞性	中譯
1. belief	n.	信仰
2. organization	n.	組織
3. graduate	n.	大學畢業生
4. tolerate	v.	忍受

倍斯特實業坊〉看版 BESTBOOK_Unit 1-22 BJ4 不解釋

作者　鄉民英文原來是醬！Internet Slang on PTT

標題　**BJ4 不解釋**

台灣鄉民流行用語「BJ4」是「不解釋」的音譯，到 2012 年時年底開始受到歡迎，因為這一個詞很好用也顯得很酷，漸漸成為一個流行用語，使用技巧如下：如果問題是大部分鄉民都應該知道的常識，「BJ4」就是字面上的意思，懶得解釋，根本不需要解釋，因為大家都知道，英文就說「no reasons」。如果有一些色情低級的「梗」(笑話)，回覆「BJ4」就是不好意思多加解釋，看得懂的人自己去體會，英文可以用「understand the meaning of behind sb's words」，除此之外「BJ4」也表達出一種不屑解釋的態度，看得懂就懂，不懂就算了，英文就說「Forget it.」算了吧！

MP3 022

Internet slang "BJ4" is a play on "need not explain" in Mandarin. The term becomes popular at the end of 2012. Since the term is **catchy** and up-to-date, it turned into a **trendy** expression as time goes by. The tips to use: if its answer of the question is widely known among the netizens, "BJ4" represents nothing more than its **literal** meaning because there is no need to explain and "no reasons". If some are **confused** about certain low-class, usually sexual jokes, reply with "BJ4" means that one is too shy to explain. The meaning behind is only left for those who can relate. In English, "understand the meaning of behind sb's words" may convey the spirit. Apart from that, "BJ4" also gives out a sense of **depreciation**. Wise ones understand, while the others do not. If you are not one of the "smarty pants", "forget it" may be a proper saying.

※發信站：「鄉民這樣說」實業坊(ptt.cc) 來自 140.115.208.44

※文章網址：https://www.ptt.cc/bbs/PttNewhand/M.1452581219.A.FAF.

→ **Kim:** Billy's acting is weird recently.

金：最近比利的舉動有點奇怪。

推 **Ryan:** How come?

雷恩：怎麼說？

→ **Kim:** He waits for me down the dorm several times and helps me out at work.

金：他常常在宿舍外等我一起上課，上班時還會時不時幫我忙。

→ **Ryan:** Maybe he has feelings for you.

雷恩：也許他對妳有好感吧。

推 **Kim:** To be honest, I feel that he acts like this to all his female friends.

金：老實說，我覺得他對每個女性朋友都這樣。

→ **Ryan:** Err....yeah, forget it.

雷恩：呃…BJ4。

單字加油站

單字	詞性	中譯
1. catchy	adj.	好聽易記的
2. trendy	adj.	流行的
3. literal	adj.	字面上的
4. confuse	v.	將…混淆，使困惑
5. depreciation	n.	輕視、不屑

倍斯特實業坊〉 看版 BESTBOOK

熱門看板	分類看板

PART 02 → 你這個人的特質吼！

倍斯特實業坊〉 看版 BESTBOOK_Unit 2-1 神人

作者 鄉民英文原來是醬！Internet Slang on PTT

標題 「神人」He is really something.

在 PPT 上「神」通常是作為動詞用，或是大部分形容一個強者或是厲害的人的形容詞。它原本由「伸手要圖片的動作」轉變而來，起源於 PPT 上的「表特版」(Beauty)，當鄉民們對於版上所討論的「表特」正妹有興趣時，要求廣大的版友協助「延伸」出更多的相片，就會用「伸」這個動詞。如果一個網友擅長「神出」正妹的更多照片，那他就是網友們的神啦！且在中文中「伸」和「神」有相似的發音，現在在台灣，稱讚特別有能力或是成功的人，就叫他們「神人」。在英文中，可用「You are / He is really something.」或是「That's impressive.」來大力稱讚別人，稱讚他人「真是個角色」。

MP3 023

"God" is originally a verb on PTT, or it is mostly an adjective called someone is brilliant and awesome. It originates from the action that somebody stretches out one's hand to ask for more pictures or the information about pretty girls who the netizens are interested in the forum "Beauty". When the hottie's pictures **go viral**, then the netizens will use the power of the netizens to accomplish the goal to search for more pictures and information about her. If one of the netizens is good at "Google" the pretty girls' pictures, then he is the God of the netizens. "**Stretching out** one's hand" and "God" share the similar **pronunciations** in Chinese. Then now in Taiwan, "God" becomes a common slang to praise someone who is successful and with a special skill. In English, people praise others with "You are really something." or "That's impressive." to tell them that they are great and special.

※發信站：「鄉民這樣說」實業坊(ptt.cc) 來自 140.115.208.44
※文章網址：https://www.ptt.cc/bbs/PttNewhand/M.1452581219.A.FAF.

→ **Hank:** Hey, did you check the latest post on the Beauty forum? There's a new picture about a very stunning girl.
嘿，你有看到表特版最新的貼文嗎?有個漂亮正妹的新照片耶。

推 **Frank:** Oh, yes! I saw the post, and many people are asking for more pictures of her. Some people are just so great with finding more information on the Internet. Their searching skills are just incredible!
喔，有!我有看到那篇貼文，有很多人已經要求更多有關她的照片，有些鄉民真的是很擅長利用網路來搜索相關訊息，他們的網路搜索技能真的很了不起!

→ **Hank:** Totally! In my mind, I really put those great searchers on a pedestal. For me personally, I am just not that patient to spend much of my time searching for things online. I'd rather do something else, to be honest with you.
真的!在我看來，這些鄉民真的是「神人」無誤，對我自己來說，我實在沒有這麼多耐心來花時間搜尋資訊，老實說我還寧願拿這時間來做別的事呢。

推 **Frank:** It's okay! We just need to rely on those good searchers anyway. See? I think more posts are just being shared right this second!
沒關係!我們只需倚賴那些「神人」等級的鄉民即可，看吧!現在馬上又有更多貼文被分享了!

單字加油站

單字	詞性	中譯
1. go viral	ph.	流行
2. stretch out	ph.	伸出(手)
3. pronunciation	n.	發音

倍斯特實業坊〉看版 BESTBOOK_Unit 2-2 屁孩

作者 鄉民英文原來是醬！Internet Slang on PTT

標題 「屁孩」Spoiled Brat

「屁孩」原本指在學齡前的孩童，因年紀小及穿著的關係，偶爾露出臀部，現在常用來形容一個大人的任性個性和我行我素的舉止，像是個不成熟的孩童一般，是一個貶義詞。在英文中，可用「spoiled brat」來表達「屁孩」這個字，其字面上即是指「被寵壞的孩子」的意思，用來形容行為舉止任性、喜愛無理取鬧的成人，就像尚未長大成熟一樣的「屁孩」行為。

MP3 024

「屁孩」 at first refers to **pre-school** kids. Due to their young age and **outfit**, sometimes they show their **butt** without noticing it. The word is then turned into a term to describe those full-grown men who still act like a kid. They are **self-centered**, and often do whatever they want without considering others, just like an immature **toddler**, and it often carries the negative meaning nowadays. In English, the word “spoiled brat” can pretty much tells the same story. The word itself simply means “a spoiled kid”. It indicates grownups who act just like childish kids.

※發信站：「鄉民這樣說」實業坊(ptt.cc) 來自 140.115.208.44
※文章網址：https://www.ptt.cc/bbs/PttNewhand/M.1452581219.A.FAF.

→ **Larry:** Did you see the news about the politician's son being drunk, making a fool of himself in the restaurant last night? What a spoiled brat!

你有看到新聞嗎?有關那位政治家兒子昨晚在餐館喝醉、鬧事的新聞?果真是個「屁孩」!

推 **Tina:** Totally! It's a shame that his father is such a respected man in the community. I guess the saying is not necessarily right, "like father like son," you know? It's really important to instill good values in children when they were growing up, not to spoil them rotten.

當然有囉!真是可惜，因為他爸爸是個社會上很受人尊敬的人啊，所以說啊，「有其父必有其子」這句話不一定是對的，是吧?所以在孩子成長過程中灌輸正確的價值觀是很重要的，而不是寵壞他們。

→ **Larry:** I totally concur. I always rule with an iron fist when it comes to demonstrating what's right and what's wrong to my own kids.

我完全同意，而對於我自己的小孩，我總是秉持著「鐵血政策」的原則來教導對錯。

單字加油站

單字	詞性	中譯
1. pre-school	adj.	學齡前的、幼稚園的
2. outfit	n.	打扮
3. butt	n.	屁股
4. self-centered	adj.	以自我為中心的
5. toddler	n.	幼童

倍斯特實業坊〉 看版 BESTBOOK_Unit 2-3 玻璃心

作者 鄉民英文原來是醬！Internet Slang on PTT

標題 「玻璃心」Too sensitive

如果有人太過敏感軟弱，無法接受任何指教，只要聽到別人批評立刻崩潰，這一種人就有顆「玻璃心」。「玻璃心」這一個詞在網路上經過轉變，用來揶揄無法討論兩岸關係的中國網友，因他們對與自己不同的意見反應過度。這些有顆玻璃心的人往往不太成熟，無法成熟面對跟自己不同的意見和批評他們的心臟就跟玻璃一樣脆弱。在英文中，會用「too sensitive」「太敏感」來形容這樣的人，太敏感的人容易心靈脆弱，有時候降卑自己，放下自尊，就能讓心更堅強。畢竟唯有打不倒你的事物，才能使你變得更剛強。

MP3 025

If one is too sensitive to take any critical feedback and always breaks down upon receiving one, then he/she certainly has a glass heart (玻璃心). The term evolved after a while on the Internet, becoming a teasing phrase for Chinese netizens who can't bear seeing any **discussion** about Cross-Strait relations. They usually **overreact** to **opposite** opinions and have little tolerant of the opposite opinions and their hearts are fragile as glass. These "glass-hearted people" tend to be **immature** and unable to handle different thoughts. In English, people refer to those who fit the description above as sensitive. Sensitive people usually have a fragile heart that is easily **shattered**. Sometimes, lower yourself and put down that ego do help the heart to be strengthened. After all, what doesn't kill you makes you stronger.

※發信站：「鄉民這樣說」實業坊(ptt.cc) 來自 140.115.208.44
※文章網址：https://www.ptt.cc/bbs/PttNewhand/M.1452581219.A.FAF.

→ **Lucy111:** Did you see the discussions on the forum? Although a few heated exchanges between users shall be deemed healthy, but some of the debates seem to be a bit melodramatic and disproportionate to the issues being discussed at hand. Most people today seem to have got a gentle soul, and can be somewhat overly sensitive to the slightest thing.
你有看到論壇上的討論嗎?雖然進行較激動的討論是好的、健康的，但有些爭論似乎有點過於戲劇性，且不相符合其討論主題的程度、嚴重性，許多現代人好像都有一顆「玻璃心」，容易對小事情有極大的反應。

推 **Tammy050:** I agreed. Just take today's latest news for example, some people are going amok on the passing of same-sex marriage equality. I don't understand why some opposing groups would go through the lengths trying to stop the laws being passed, and display such hatred in public?
我同意，就以今天的新聞為例好了，許多人對於同性婚姻的合法化有很多意見，我不明白為什麼反對的團體會這麼耗費精力地來阻止立法，並在大庭廣眾下展現仇恨?

單字加油站

單字	詞性	中譯
1. discussion	n.	討論
2. overreact	v.	反應過度
3. opposite	adj.	相反的
4. immature	adj.	不成熟的
5. shatter	v.	粉碎、砸碎

倍斯特實業坊〉看版 BESTBOOK_Unit 2-4 鄉民

作者 鄉民英文原來是醬！Internet Slang on PTT

標題 「鄉民」the netizen

「鄉民」，顧名思義原本是用來指來自鄉下的民眾，而隨著網際網路的發達，一開始是用來形容 PTT 上「黑特版」的一些喜歡湊熱鬧、喜愛分享謬論的網友，帶有負面的意思。這個字形容花很多時間上網的人，現今的「鄉民」一詞，隨著社會脈動的進展，已儼然成為台灣流行的網路論壇 PTT 上網友的代稱，現在較無一開始的負面意涵；在英文中，用來形容「鄉民」的字詞，最直接的字詞是「netizen」，是將網路的「Internet」這個單字與公民「citizen」結合。

MP3 026

The netizens in Chinese **translates** into “the people from the country” literally, since it originally means a bunch of people who like to **join the crowd** and share **misinformation** on the forum. It describes those who spend lots of time on Internet. Now because of the development of the Internet, this term becomes widely used and is the other name of the netizens on the popular forum, PTT in Taiwan. Now it turns into a **neutral** noun. In English, the word “the netizen” means the person who uses the Internet, and it is derived from the combination of two words “Internet” and “citizen”.

※發信站：「鄉民這樣說」實業坊(ptt.cc) 來自 140.115.208.44
※文章網址：https://www.ptt.cc/bbs/PttNewhand/M.1452581219.A.FAF.

→ **Greg:** Hey, how are you? Long time no see! It's been quite a while since last talking to you!

嘿，你好嗎?好久不見!上次看到你是好久以前的事了!

推 **Jimmy:** Yeah! Where have you been? What's been going on with you? I have no idea what you're up to these days. You don't update the latest adventures of yours on social media no more. It's hard to reach you, you know?

對呀，你去哪了?最近在做什麼呀?我都不知道你最近在搞什麼玩意兒，你也不在社群網站上分享你最新的資訊了，很難聯繫你呀，你知道嗎?

→ **Greg:** Yes, I'm not as an active netizen as the the most people are. Hey, but I know every single thing you're up to every single day.

是啊，我不像大部分的人一樣，是個活躍的「鄉民」，嘿，但我可知道你每天在做什麼。

推 **Jimmy:** You got me, bro! I'm the total opposite of you. I like to share everything on social media.

兄弟，被你發現了!我跟你完全相反，我喜歡在社群網站上分享所有資訊。

單字加油站

單字	詞性	中譯
1. translate	v.	翻譯
2. misinformation	n.	錯誤的資訊
3. neutral	adj.	中性的
4. join the crowd	ph.	湊熱鬧
5. forum	n.	網路論壇

倍斯特實業坊〉 看版 BESTBOOK_Unit 2-5 頗呵

作者 鄉民英文原來是醬！Internet Slang on PTT

標題 「頗呵」Ridiculous

網路用語「頗呵」是指某件事或某個人的行為挺有趣的滑稽的，「呵」的來源是注音文「ㄏ」，一開始在網路上較常出現「ㄏㄏ」來表達「呵呵笑」的意思，後來逐漸發展成「頗呵」來形容某人的舉動讓人無法理解，想呵呵笑因為有點尷尬的意思。在英文中，可用單詞「ridiculous」、「laughable」形容一個人的行為舉止「頗呵」，但「ridiculous」用一個字簡單表達跟「頗呵」比較相似，或是片語「laughing my socks off」形容一件事或某人的行為太滑稽，讓人笑到不能自已，笑到襪子都掉了！

MP3 027

The slang 「頗呵」 means something or someone's action are very funny and ridiculous. The origin of 「呵」 is zhuyin and 「ㄏㄏ」 is widely used in the first place online to show one's laughter. Then it gradually turns into the description towards the weird actions that makes people confused and laugh, with a little bit embarrassed.

In English, you can use "ridiculous" and "laughable" to describe some funny actions and behaviors, or the phrase "laughing my socks off", which means one thing or one's behavior is so hilarious that make you laugh loud and even your socks off.

※發信站：「鄉民這樣說」實業坊(ptt.cc) 來自 140.115.208.44
※文章網址：https://www.ptt.cc/bbs/PttNewhand/M.1452581219.A.FAF.

→ **Sherry:** Did you see the last night's comedic show on TV?
你有看昨晚電視播放的喜劇嗎?

推 **Maggie:** Yes, I did! Did you see the part where the politician made a special appearance in the cow costumes? That part is ridiculous!
有呀!你有看到那個政治人物穿乳牛裝特串的部分嗎?那部分實在是「頗呵」!

→ **Sherry:** Yes, I laughed my socks off during those scenes where the politician played the cameo role, especially the final scene where he accidentally slipped on the banana peels.
對呀，那政治人物特串演出的部分真是「頗呵」，讓我笑的不能自己，尤其是最後他不小心踩到香蕉皮滑倒的場景。

推 **Maggie:** It's interesting to see someone who's quite serious in his day-to-day jobs loosen up a bit. People can definitely relate to him more after seeing the episode.
能夠看到平常工作嚴肅的人放開表演，還蠻有趣的，百姓看完這集後，絕對更能接受他。

單字加油站

單字	詞性	中譯
1. laughter	n.	笑聲
2. description	n.	形容
3. confused	adj.	疑惑的
4. behavior	n.	行為
5. hilarious	adj.	非常滑稽的

倍斯特實業坊〉 看版 BESTBOOK_Unit 2-6 媽寶

作者 鄉民英文原來是醬！Internet Slang on PTT

標題 「媽寶」Mama's Boy

「媽寶」這一個詞帶有貶意，是媽媽寶貝的縮寫。形容已經成年，卻少有自己主見的兒子。這種人以母親的意見為中心，每天的瑣事都依賴媽媽關切和打理。無論決定或大或小，他們絕對會先問媽媽再說。通常所謂的媽寶缺乏自主的能力，他們無法獨立思考、沒有責任感且難以接受挫折。一言以敝之，他們就是還像一個小孩一般依賴著媽媽。另一個類似的詞「daddy's girl」則是用來形容女兒是父親的掌上明珠。

MP3 028

Mama's boy is a negative term, which stands for "Mommy's baby boy". The term usually indicates grown-up men who don't really have their own opinions. Instead, they take their mom's **suggestions** all the time and depend very much on mommy's loving care for their **daily** life. Every decision, big or small, they would not make without **consulting** their moms. The so-called mama's boy has a lack of **independency**. They can't think on their own, refuse to take on responsibility, and normally aren't good at dealing with **frustrations**. In a word, mama's boy relies on their mother like a toddler. Another term "daddy's girl" conveys the similar meaning, which means baby girls of their daddies.

※發信站：「鄉民這樣說」實業坊(ptt.cc) 來自 140.115.208.44
※文章網址：https://www.ptt.cc/bbs/PttNewhand/M.1452581219.A.FAF.

→ **Steven:** Hey, how's your younger brother doing? Is he still living at home with your parents?

嘿，你弟弟最近如何?他還跟你爸媽一起住家裡嗎?

推 **Tiffany:** Of course, how can he not? He's such a mama's boy. My mother would take care of him with everything, from preparing home-cooked meals to doing his laundry. He staying at home, without a care in the world, is not going to change anytime soon.

他當然還住家裡囉，他真是個「媽寶」，我媽媽總是將他照顧的無微不至的，從三餐的準備到洗衣服，他皆不用操心，所以這狀況短期內是不會變的。

→ **Steven:** That's nice. How about you? Although you're such a daddy's girl, you'd prefer to get your own place, right?

真好! 那你呢? 儘管你也是爸爸的掌上明珠，你較傾向在外面有個自己的家，是吧?

推 **Tiffany:** Yeah, I am much more independent than my brother, you know.

對，我比我弟弟獨立自主多了，你知道的。

單字加油站

單字	詞性	中譯
1. suggestion	n.	建議
2. daily	adj.	每天的
3. consult	v.	商量
4. independency	n.	獨立自主
5. frustration	n.	挫折

倍斯特實業坊〉 看版 BESTBOOK_Unit 2-7 啃老族

作者 鄉民英文原來是醬！Internet Slang on PTT

標題 「啃老族」 NEET

「啃老族」 是形容在生活上無法經濟獨立(not financially independent)的年輕族群，成年了還無所事事，依賴父母的贊助及支持生活。在英文中，有所謂的「NEET」，中文為「尼特族」「Not in Employment, Education or Training」的縮寫，即為不急於就業、求學或受專業職業訓練的青年。而在日本也出現「parasite single」(單身寄生族)一詞，跟「NEET」有相似的意思，指已經成年和從學校畢業的單身男女，但沒有固定工作，且還住在家中不急於成家立業的年輕人。

MP3 029

In Chinese,「啃老族」is a group of young people who cannot live **financially independent**, and they are adult but still depend on their parents to **support** their lives. In English, a NEET is a person who is "Not in Employment, **Education** or Training" is not seeking jobs, not enrolled in school or work-related training. In Japan, there is a word "parasite single" which shares the similar meaning as a NEET, and this **classification** means the grownup and graduated single youngsters are out of work, seeking for jobs and still live home. Apparently they are not ready to leave home and have own family and career.

※發信站：「鄉民這樣說」實業坊(ptt.cc) 來自 140.115.208.44
※文章網址：https://www.ptt.cc/bbs/PttNewhand/M.1452581219.A.FAF.

→ **Marvin:** Hey, Dorothy, how are you? How are your children doing? It's been ages since I saw them last time. If I remember correctly, they're now in their mid-twenties, right?

嘿，桃樂絲，最近好嗎?孩子們最近如何?我好久沒看到他們了，如果我沒記錯的話，他們應該已經二十幾歲了吧?

推 **Dorothy:** Hi, Marvin! My children and I are doing great! You're right. They're in their mid-twenties now. It's amazing how time fly in the blink of an eye. Now they're working in different cities. Sometimes I hope they're NEET, so that I can enjoy their companion every single day.

嗨，馬文!我跟孩子們過得都好!你說的對，他們現在都二十幾歲了，時間可真的是一眨眼就過了，他們現在各自在不同的城市工作，有時候我真希望他們是尼特族、「啃老族」，這樣我就能每天跟他們相處了!

→ **Marvin:** I think that's many parents' inner secret, right?

我猜想這是許多父母內心深處的願望，對吧?

單字加油站

單字	詞性	中譯
1. financially	adv.	經濟地
2. independent	adj.	獨立的
3. support	v.	支持
4. education	n.	教育
5. classification	n.	分類

倍斯特實業坊〉看版 BESTBOOK_Unit 2-8 水水

作者 鄉民英文原來是醬！Internet Slang on PTT

標題 「水水」 Gorgeous

網路上，台灣網友們用「水水」一詞來稱呼 PPT或其它論壇上的女性網友，尤其是在美妝或醫美等女性看板上，常看到女網友們使用「水水」這個暱稱來互相稱呼，表示友好和禮貌，就像中國的網友會用「親」在網路上互相稱呼來展現親切和友善的感覺。它的緣由來自台語「水噹噹」、「水水」等形容女性貌美的字。在英文中，可用「gorgeous」(漂亮的)，是一個比「beautiful」或是「pretty」 更常見的單字，常見讚美女生外表的句子會說「You are gorgeous！」，或是直接稱呼美女為「a gorgeous」。

MP3 030

Taiwanes netizens call the other girls in the name of “water” in Chinese on PTT and the other forums, especially on the **cosmetic** and **plastic surgery** forums. Girls call each other “water” in Chinese to being **friendly** and polite, like netizens in China call each other “dear” online to show their **goodwill** and politeness. And “water” originates from the Taiwanese word to describe a girl’s beauty. In English, people call the beauty “gorgeous” which is a more common word to **praise** a girl’s beauty than “beautiful” and “pretty” in daily life. “You are gorgeous!” is a common sentence to praise a girl’ appearance in English, and they just call a pretty girl as “a gorgeous”.

※發信站：「鄉民這樣說」實業坊(ptt.cc) 來自 140.115.208.44
※文章網址：https://www.ptt.cc/bbs/PttNewhand/M.1452581219.A.FAF.
(On the MakeUp forum 在美妝版)

→ **Host:** Good afternoon, gorgeous! Welcome, welcome! Thank you for joining our workshops for today. We'll be introducing some of the latest beauty products to y'all, and share some of the practical tips on how to apply makeup without hassle on a busy working day. Do you have any questions?
各位「水水」午安!歡迎、歡迎!謝謝各位加入我們今天舉辦的工作坊，我們會介紹一些最新的美妝產品給各位，並分享一些有用的技巧，教大家如何在忙碌的生活中也能輕鬆上妝，那各位目前有什麼問題嗎？

推 **Participant** A: I'd like to acquire some useful tips on how I can quickly put on makeup on a busy workday and look professional.
我想學習如何能夠在忙碌的工作天，也能快速上妝，維持專業的外表。

→**Host:** Then you're definitely in the right place! Our next guest speaker will demonstrate how with a little bit of makeup, you can be instantly tuning heads with your rare beauty.
那妳就來對地方了!我們的下一位客座講師將會示範，如何藉由一點淡妝，就能立即讓各位「水水」充滿吸引力。

單字加油站

單字	詞性	中譯
1. cosmetic	n.	化妝
2. plastic surgery	n.	整形手術
3. friendly	adj.	友善的
4. goodwill	n.	善意
5. praise	v.	稱讚

倍斯特實業坊〉看版 BESTBOOK_Unit 2-9 魯蛇

作者	鄉民英文原來是醬！Internet Slang on PTT
標題	「魯蛇」Loser

「魯蛇」來自網路論壇 PTT，源自英文輸家(loser)的意思。有一些人喜歡在網路上酸、諷刺別人的成就和成功是因為身家顯赫，而非因為自己的努力，因此一段時間之後，開始有人譏諷這些「酸民」為「魯蛇」。魯蛇這麼愛酸別人，其實是因為他們內心感到自卑。有些人也會用魯蛇自嘲，因為相對於人生勝利組「the whole package」，剛畢業的社會新鮮人，沒什麼非凡的成就或是單身的人，就像是個人生輸家，所以自我解嘲是一條魯蛇。英文有個片語 has nothing going for oneself，意思就是某一個人沒有什麼特別的成就。

MP3 031

The saying 「魯蛇」 comes from Internet forum PTT. It is a Chinese taken on the English word "loser" who doesn't win the game. There are haters online who love to tease that some people make achievement and have success only because their family **background** or the **wealth**, not because their effort. After a while, the sarcastic saying "loser" starts to come to use for calling those who are only good at mocking at other people. The reason why these people like to tease others is actually because of their **inferior** feelings. Sometimes people also use the word to **make fun of** self, compared with the whole package, those who are fresh **graduated** and have nothing to be bragged about or are single are like losers of life. In English, there's a phrase "has nothing going for oneself", indicating that someone doesn't have any achievement in particular, whereas loves to criticize others for being successful.

※發信站：「鄉民這樣說」實業坊(ptt.cc) 來自 140.115.208.44

※文章網址：https://www.ptt.cc/bbs/PttNewhand/M.1452581219.A.FAF.

→ **Teresa：** Hey, congratulations on your hit single! I love your interpretation of the song. You're really the hottest female artist on the music scene right now.

嘿，恭喜妳單曲的成功啊!我很喜歡妳對於歌曲的詮釋，妳真的是當今音樂界最火紅的女歌手啊。

推 **Singer:** Oh, thank you so much for the compliment. You really like it? I guess I just got a bit derailed by some negative comments about the song on the Internet today. That's why I was thinking maybe it's not good enough.

喔，真是謝謝妳的稱讚，妳真的喜歡這首歌嗎？謝謝，我猜我是被今天網路上一些有關這首歌的負面評論給分心了，所以我開始在想或許這首歌還有很多進步的空間。

→ **Teresa:** Ignore those comments. Those are from the losers who have nothing going for themselves. That's why they're so hateful.

別理會那些評論，那些都是沒什麼事好做的「魯蛇」們所留下的評論，正因為他們沒什麼正事好做，才會如此厭惡別人的成就!

單字加油站

單字	詞性	中譯
1. background	n.	背景
2. wealth	n.	財富
3. inferior	adj.	次等的
4. make fun of		開某人玩笑
5. graduate	v.	畢業

倍斯特實業坊〉看版 BESTBOOK_Unit 2-10 丁丁、腦殘	
作者	鄉民英文原來是醬！Internet Slang on PTT
標題	「丁丁、腦殘」Someone has a screw loose

網路上可常看見鄉民使用「丁丁」這個詞來描述某人的言論或行為很蠢，類似「腦殘」的意思，源自於英國幼教節目—天線寶寶(Teletubbies)，節目內角色總是重複地一樣的話及做一樣的動作，讓一般大人看這個節目時，感到「丁丁」等寶寶們的行為很白癡、腦殘，久而發展成鄉民流行用語。丁丁的原名為「Tinky Winky」，是「天線寶寶」四個主角中紫色、頭上有個倒三角造型的角色。在英文中，可用「Someone has a screw loose.」來形容「丁丁」和「腦殘」般的行為，好像腦內似乎有根螺絲鬆了，比喻其言論或行為怪異、不正常，也可用「Someone is not all there.」來描述。

MP3 032

Taiwanese netizens often use “Tinky Winky”「丁丁」to describe someone is dumb or acts in a stupid way. Tinky Winky originates from the British TV show “Teletubbies”, the **character** Tinky Winky is a purple bear-like figure with an upside-down triangle on his head. Acting silly and repeating the same thing over and over again makes Tinky Winky a little **weird**, funny and silly. This general **perception** of the character soon passes onto cyber world, where people start calling others Tinky Winky **in place of** stupid. English idiom “someone has a screw loose” could fit perfectly into this circumstance. If one’s brain has a screw loose, then he/she must not be acting normally or **reasonably**, therefore acting like a Tinky Winky. “Someone is not all there” also shares the same meaning.

※發信站：「鄉民這樣說」實業坊(ptt.cc) 來自 140.115.208.44
※文章網址：https://www.ptt.cc/bbs/PttNewhand/M.1452581219.A.FAF.

→ **Tom:** Did you tune in for the presidential election debate last night?
妳有觀看昨晚的總統大選辯論直播嗎？

推 **Grace:** Of course, I would not miss it for the world. It's quite an intense debate amongst the candidates, isn't it?
當然囉，我是不會錯過的，昨晚的辯論真是激烈啊!

→ **Tom:** Yes, but in all honesty, I can't really fathom the Republican candidate's way of thinking on how to restore the current economy.
是的，但老實說，我實在是搞不懂那位共和黨候選人所提出有關恢復經濟的論點。

推 **Grace:** I agree, and he's gotten quite some flack in the media as many political analysts describe him as having a screw loose. But still, he's somehow able to come out ahead in the polls these days.
對呀，他最近也被媒體強烈抨擊，許多政治研究員甚至稱他為「丁丁」、「腦殘」，但他在最近的民調中還是拔得頭籌。

→ **Tom:** So when it comes to politics, you just never know, right?
所以只要是有關政治，任何事都可能發生，是吧？

單字加油站

單字	詞性	中譯
1. character	n.	角色
2. weird	adj.	古怪的
3. perception	n.	觀點
4. in place of		取代
5. reasonably	adv.	合理地

倍斯特實業坊〉 看版 BESTBOOK_Unit 2-11 小白

作者	鄉民英文原來是醬！Internet Slang on PTT
標題	「小白」 Internet Troll; Rookie, Noob, Newbie

由於「小白」這個字詞一開始是用來形容某人不遵守 PTT 的規矩、喜歡發好戰、負面的發文等不受控的網路行為，進而引發網路論戰的網友，而隨著「小白」一詞的演化，現在較無一開始的負面意思，而是用來指稱新人或菜鳥的意思，因此可用英文中的「Rookie」、「Noob」、「Newbie」指新手或初學者，但現在通常是用來指某一個論壇或領域的菜鳥、新手，不像以前形容某人不守規矩、有白目行為的負面意思。

MP3 033

This term is originally used to describe someone who is very **out of bounds** and **behaves** badly in an **idiotic** way on the Internet and likes to post the negative comments to cause **arguments**. In other words, they are the kind of Internet users who do not **abide** by certain rules of the Internet forum. But now it's generally used to refer to someone who is new to a certain forum or a field such as, Rookie, Noob, Newbie.

※發信站：「鄉民這樣說」實業坊(ptt.cc) 來自 140.115.208.44
※文章網址：https://www.ptt.cc/bbs/PttNewhand/M.1452581219.A.FAF.

→ **Judy:** Look! My new iPhone X has face recognition! Now I don't even need to use a finger to unlock it!

茱蒂：你看！我的新 iPhone X 有臉部辨識功能耶！現在我連碰都不用碰就能解鎖手機了！

推 **Ryan:** Come on, Newbie! You know it now? I've had my iPhone XR as soon as it came out!

雷恩：拜託，妳是新手喔，現在才知道？iPhone XR 一出我就立馬敗了好不好！

→ **Judy:** Wow, Mr. Know-It-All, I'm not an Apple fan like you! How dare you call me like that?

茱蒂：是喔，這麼行？我又不像你是果粉！幹嘛叫我新手？

推 **Ryan:** There are many more new features. Watch and learn, rookie!

雷恩：還有很多新功能喔，學著點啊，菜鳥！

單字加油站

單字	詞性	中譯
1. behave	v.	行為
2. idiotic	adj.	愚蠢的
3. argument	n.	爭論
4. abide	v.	不能忍受
5. out of bounds	ph.	在界外...

倍斯特實業坊〉 看版 BESTBOOK_Unit 2-12 貓奴	
作者	鄉民英文原來是醬！Internet Slang on PTT
標題	「貓奴」A Cat Person

「貓奴」，顧名思義就是貓的奴隸，狹義的貓奴是指飼養貓咪的人，現在的貓咪飼主甘願為自己的貓做牛做馬，他們的地位好像在貓咪之下，像奴才般服侍著自己的主子們。讓人誤以為貓才是主人，而飼養貓的人像是服侍貓咪的僕人一般，他們被稱作「貓奴」。另外一種類型的「貓奴」是他們沒有養貓當寵物，但是他們依然對所有貓咪的事物很有熱情，花很多時間和精力去了解他們愛的動物。現在有越來越多的人將寵物視為生命中很重要的部分，所以這一個詞變得很流行。在英文中常會聽到有人問「Are you a cat person or dog person?」，當聽到有人形容自己是「a cat person」，表示自己是非常喜歡貓咪的。

MP3 034

「貓奴」in a narrow sense is usually defined as the pet owners who love their cats and take care of them very well, or in general, they are a group of people who are crazy about anything related to cats. People in Taiwan call those people serves their cats like their masters as "cat servants" in Chinese. These cat persons take care of their cats in great details and they exchange the roles, so the cat becomes the masters waiting for their good service. Another type of the cat person is they may not own a cat as pets, but they are still very passionate about cats and are willing to dedicate time and efforts to learn more about their beloved **feline** animal. Nowadays, people spend more time on their pets and see their pets as one important part of their life, so this term becomes very popular. In English, people will ask "Are you a cat person or dog person?" or people describe themselves as "cat person" to show their affection to cats.

※發信站：「鄉民這樣說」實業坊(ptt.cc) 來自 140.115.208.44
※文章網址：https://www.ptt.cc/bbs/PttNewhand/M.1452581219.A.FAF.

→ **Tim:** Henry, do you have any plans for the weekend? Wanna check something out at the newly opened shopping **plaza**? I heard they have so many interesting shops.

亨利，週末有什麼計畫嗎?要不要去新開的購物廣場逛逛，聽說有許多有趣的商店喔。

推 **Henry:** Sounds great, but NO. I am gonna stay home because it's caturday! I need to spend some **quality time** with my cats at home.

聽起來不錯，不過我想要在家裡休息，好好享受「貓咪星期六」!我要好好與我親愛的寵物貓們共享歡樂時光。

→ **Tim:** Huh? What? Don't really get the words that you cat lovers are using? What's a caturday?

什麼？我實在不懂你們這些「貓奴」所用的字詞，什麼是「貓咪星期六」啊？

推 **Henry:** Oh I forgot you're more of a dog person instead of a cat person. Let me explain. A caturday can refer to any day off from work, and you get to relax at home just like what a cat normally does!

喔，我忘記你比較喜歡狗，不是個「貓奴」，讓我解釋一下，「貓咪星期六」可用來指任何假日，因為你可以像貓一樣在家慵懶的休息、享受。

單字加油站

單字	詞性	中譯
1. feline	a.	貓科的
2. plaza	n.	廣場
3. quality time	n.	優質、歡樂時光

作者 鄉民英文原來是醬！Internet Slang on PTT

標題 「中肯」Hit the nail on the head

「中肯」是稱讚網友很誠實且網反的意見正中要點的一個形容詞，因為用字簡潔，所以非常受歡迎也在生活和網路中被廣泛的使用。「中肯」是用來指一個人所說的話切中核心，沒有特別拐彎抹角又精闢，通常是用來稱讚發言所言甚是、一針見血，常常可以在留言區看到鄉民在一篇文章回覆寫「原 po 中肯」和「樓上中肯」表示對文章的贊同，與臉書中的「按讚」一樣的意思。

MP3 035

「中肯」the term means someone is very honest, and their opinions **cut straight to the core**. These two words are simple to use so this term is very popular and is widely-used either in real life or on Internet forums. There are many idioms in English to describe that someone's words or opinions are a true and honest **depiction** of reality. One term that we often hear is the use of "hit the nail on the head." It is used to describe that someone says something that is to the point, exactly what the situation is at hand. It is commonly used and seen on the PTT, and the netizens will reply 「中肯」on the post to show their agreement and support to the posts, like giving other a like on Facebook.

※發信站：「鄉民這樣說」實業坊(ptt.cc) 來自 140.115.208.44
※文章網址：https://www.ptt.cc/bbs/PttNewhand/M.1452581219.A.FAF.

→ **Tiffany:** Did you see the **op-ed** written by George on the newspaper yesterday? His opinions on the **incumbent governor** hit the nail on the head, don't you think?
你有看到昨天報紙中喬治寫的社論嗎？我覺得他對於現任州長的評論很「中肯」，你覺得呢？

推 **Jason:** I agree. He talks about the governor not living up to his promises during his **campaign**. In reality, the governor really doesn't.
我同意，他提到州長沒有實現他選舉期間的諾言，而事實上，州長的確沒有實現他的諾言。

→ **Tiffany:** Right, like the governor talked about **reviving** the state's economy, but so far after 2 years, the economy hasn't improved. Instead, statistics have shown that the economy has worsened by 0.25 percent.
對呀，我記得州長原本說要復甦經濟，但兩年後，經濟仍未見起色，而現有數據反而指出經濟退步了 0.25 個百分比。

單字加油站

單字	詞性	中譯
1. cut straight to the core		切中核心、重點
2. depiction	n.	描述
3. op-ed	n.	社論文章
4. incumbent	adj.	現任的、在任的
5. governor	n.	州長、統治者
6. campaign	n.	選舉、造勢活動
7. revive	v.	復甦、振興

倍斯特實業坊〉 看版 BESTBOOK_Unit 2-14 太狂了

作者 鄉民英文原來是醬！Internet Slang on PTT

標題 「太狂了！」It's lit.

Lit 的意思原本是用來形容某人微醺、過嗨，因為使用藥物或酒精的關係所造成，進而演化成形容某人或某事很厲害、很嗨、很令人興奮、好玩等正面意含，「狂」，在網友的意思裡就是太猛了、太厲害了，不過在網友各種發展之下，「太狂了吧」逐漸也衍生諷刺和揶揄的意思，隨著廣泛地使用，有時也會被用來諷刺某人或某事，表示一件事情讓某人無法接受。另外在國外網路論壇上，也常看到「litaf」這個用語，其意思也與「太狂了!」一樣，就是用來表現出讚嘆，而「af」是「as fuck」的縮寫，是年輕人常用的用法。

MP3 036

"Lit" in English is originally used to describe someone who is intoxicated, either by drugs or alcohol. Now it can be used to describe something or someone, usually a party that is fun and exciting. You can use "It's lit." to generally refer to things that are great. It's used for things that are beyond the scope of normal comprehension, things that inspire admiration and exclamation from either the participants or bystanders. In foreign Internet forums, "litaf" this word is common, and it carries the same meaning as "It is lit." to express someone's surprise. The "af" is the abbreviation of "as fuck" an expression generally used by teenagers.

※發信站：「鄉民這樣說」實業坊(ptt.cc) 來自 140.115.208.44
※文章網址：https://www.ptt.cc/bbs/PttNewhand/M.1452581219.A.FAF.

→ **Alicia151:** How's last night concert?
昨晚的演場會好玩嗎？

推 **Sam5566:** The concert is amazing. I can't believe I am finally able to hear the **international** singer sing so many of his **hit songs** in person. And the **choreography** is also very cool. All in all, it's just lit.
昨晚的演唱會很讚，我不敢相信我終於現場聽了這位國際巨星演唱他的諸多流行金曲，而且他的編舞舞蹈也很酷，總的來說，整個演唱會真是「太狂啦！」。

→ **Alicia151:** Are there any special guests perform with the singer?
有其他特別來賓與這位歌星同台演出嗎?

推 **Sam5566:** Yes, there's an **unexpected** singer who flew all the way from the states to perform with him on stage for a couple of songs. The audience was just so stoked about this pleasant surprise. Again, the whole night is just lit af.
有，有個特地從美國飛來的特別來賓與他一同演唱了幾首歌，觀眾們對這個驚喜都非常地興奮，真的，整個夜晚實在就是「太狂啦!」。

單字加油站

單字	詞性	中譯
1. international	adj.	國際的
2. hit song		流行金曲、為人知的歌曲
3. choreography	n.	舞蹈
4. unexpected	adj.	意外的

倍斯特實業坊〉 看版 BESTBOOK_Unit 2-15 海巡署

作者	鄉民英文原來是醬！Internet Slang on PTT
標題	「海巡署/住海邊」 Busybody

當你問一個人「你家住海邊喔？」，意思是指別人多管閒事，因為海是無邊無際的。這是一個有趣的說法，當覺得一個人很雞婆和愛管閒事時，便可以問他「你住海邊嗎？」來暗示對方的問題已經逾矩，侵犯到個人隱私，英文「busybody」用來形容某人愛管閒事、參與太多不關自己的事情，也可用片語「stick someone's nose in something」，而當你覺得某人的行為管太多，有「住海邊/海巡署」的嫌疑時，可以對他說「mind your own business」、「none of your business」、「butt out」。

MP3 037

When people ask you "Do you live near the sea?"「住海邊」 in Taiwan, mean the one always stick his or her nose in other's business. It is a funny way to tell people they are too nosy. The sea is wide and the one live near the sea always like get involved in other people's stuff or too interested in what other people are doing. Taiwanese will say this when they feel insulted and hint those questions are too personal and invading one's privacy. **In other words,** busybody is not the kind of person who just minds his or her business, but rather very much likes to **get involved in** other people's stuff. In America, people will "Mind your own business.", "None of your business." or "Butt out." those frank phrases to ask people not to stick their nose in others' business.

※發信站：「鄉民這樣說」實業坊(ptt.cc) 來自 140.115.208.44

※文章網址：https://www.ptt.cc/bbs/PttNewhand/M.1452581219.A.FAF.

→ **Eva621:** How's the first date last night?

昨晚的頭一次約會順利嗎?

推 **Megan219:** The conversation went great. I think we had a connection.

還 ok，還聊得來，我想我們還算來電。

→ **Eva**：**How** do you know him? Through the Internet?

你是怎麼認識他的呢？網路交友嗎？

→ **Eva:** Hope you don't find me as a busybody, but I'm **curious** if this is the first date you have with someone from the Internet?

希望你不覺得我「住海邊」，但我很好奇昨晚是你第一次與網路交友的對象約會嗎?

單字加油站

單字	詞性	中譯
1. In other words		換句話說
2. get involved in something		參與、干涉某事
3. to be honest		老實說
4. potential	adj.	潛在的、有潛力的
5. curious	adj.	好奇的

倍斯特實業坊〉看版 BESTBOOK_Unit 2-16 爆肝

作者　鄉民英文原來是醬！Internet Slang on PTT

標題　「爆肝」Pull an All-Nighter、Burn the Midnight Oil

「爆肝」是形容人非常疲勞，好像肝都要爆掉了，通常是指耗費大量的時間和精力，甚至晚上不睡熬夜工作，這一個字常跟熬夜和工作繁重有關聯。這一個詞源自於民眾認為熬夜與猛爆性肝炎（Fulminant Hepatitis）有關聯，中國人認為肝的健康與一個人健康的生活作息相關，所以晚上不睡覺會傷害肝臟的健康。因為長期熬夜所累積的疲累，都會增加身體和肝臟的負荷，最終引發猛爆性肝炎。簡單來說，「爆肝」就是形容熬夜工作，非常疲勞的樣子，工作到肝都要爆掉了。在英文中，可用「pull an all-nighter」、「burn the midnight oil」指一個人熬夜，或是較口語化的「stay up late」。

MP3 038

The Taiwanese slang 「exploding liver」is used to describe a very tired person feel their livers are going to explode because of the heavy workload. Usually it relates to no sleep at night to work and someone spend lots of time and energy on work. This word originates from Chinese belief that staying up late often causes Fulminant Hepatitis. Chinese believe that a regular life style is the key of a healthy liver, so staying up late will hurt your liver. The long term fatigue will hurt people's body and liver and eventually leads to Fulminant Hepatitis. In short, "exploding liver" means staying up late and being tired because the workload is so heavy that his/her liver is going to explode. In English, "pull an all-nighter" and "burns the midnight oil" mean doing something all night and no sleep, and "stay up late" is more common term in speaking.

※發信站：「鄉民這樣說」實業坊(ptt.cc) 來自 140.115.208.44
※文章網址：https://www.ptt.cc/bbs/PttNewhand/M.1452581219.A.FAF.

→ **Sam133:** Have you finished the **paper** due on Friday?
星期五要交的報告你完成了嗎？

推 **Dale2233:** Not yet. Oh my god, I totally forgot it. Looks like I need to pull an all-nighter to make it in time.
還沒，天啊，我整個忘了，看來我必須熬夜「爆肝」才來得及了。

→ **Sam133:** I don't think you need to burn the midnight oil, as there are still a couple of days before the deadline. As you're very familiar with the topic, I'm sure you can **whip up** a **well-organized**, **incisive** paper in no time.
你不用熬夜「爆肝」啦，還有幾天才是報告截止日，而且你對這次的題目很熟悉，我相信你一定很快就能寫出一份架構完整又精闢的報告。

推 **Dale2233:** Hope so. I really don't like staying up late. As so many studies have **pointed out**, it's bad for our health if we pull an all-nighter too often.
希望如此，要不然我真的不太想熬夜「爆肝」，就像許多研究所說的，如果太頻繁地熬夜「爆肝」是有害健康的。

單字加油站

單字	詞性	中譯
1. paper	n.	紙、報告
2. whip up	ph.	快速做出、完成
3. well-organized	adj.	架構完整、清楚的；整理完善的
4. incisive	adj.	精闢的
5. point out	ph.	指出、說出

倍斯特實業坊〉 看版 BESTBOOK_Unit 2-17 小鮮肉

作者 鄉民英文原來是醬！Internet Slang on PTT

標題 「小鮮肉」 the Stud Muffin、Young Hunk

「小鮮肉」是用來讚美體格強壯且年輕帥氣的男生，「小」和「鮮」特別是指「年輕」的帥氣男生。在英文中，可以用「stud muffin」，而用「muffin」(馬芬)這個單字傳達出對女生來說，很有吸引力又年輕帥氣的男性，就像馬芬般地可口「hunk」(猛男)，前面加上形容詞「young」(年輕的)來傳達出「小鮮肉」的意思。另外一個與這個字有關連的字是英文「cougar」，原本是美洲獅的意思，後來被引申為與比她小年輕許多的男性交往的「熟女」。

MP3 039

The term “Young Hunk” and “Stud Muffin” are used to refer to men who are especially good-looking and young. In Chinese, the term has the connotation of a young man so good-looking and attractive that he seems very delicious like a juicy steamed meat bun in English. Another word connects with “young hunk” and stud muffin is a “cougar” which means one kind puma, a large brown wild cat that lives in North and South America. Now this word also is used to describe the middle-age woman who dates a much younger man.

※發信站：「鄉民這樣說」實業坊(ptt.cc) 來自 140.115.208.44
※文章網址：https://www.ptt.cc/bbs/PttNewhand/M.1452581219.A.FAF.

→ **Anna:** Now it's **graduation season**. It's the time of the year where we're gonna see many fresh new faces in the company again.
又到了畢業季啦，公司內又會開始看到許多新的、稚嫩的面孔了。

推 **Cathy:** That's great for you. I heard from HR that there are many stud-muffins **applying for** the **positions** at our company this year. Good for you unmarried people, you need to **seize** this opportunity!
你可有福了，我聽人資部門說今年有許多「小鮮肉」應徵我們公司的職缺，你們這些未婚人可要把握機會！

→ **Anna:** Really? Let's go to HR to ask if we can take a quick look of the candidates' profile pictures. Is this **unethical**? haha.
真的嗎？那我們去人資部門問一下，看能不能快速瀏覽這些應徵者的大頭照，這樣會不會不太道德呀？哈哈

單字加油站

單字	詞性	中譯
1. graduation season		畢業季
2. apply for		申請
3. position	n.	位置、職缺
4. seize	v.	抓住、把握
5. unethical	adj.	不道德的

倍斯特實業坊〉 看版 BESTBOOK_Unit 2-18 發好人卡

作者 鄉民英文原來是醬！Internet Slang on PTT

標題 「發好人卡」 In the Friendzone

「發好人卡」指被其暗戀對象委婉拒絕時使用，在台灣，當人想要拒絕異性的追求時，常會先說「你是個好人，但…」來當開場，希望用不傷害別人的方式委婉拒絕，這就是這一詞的起源，為了讓被拒絕的人不要太傷心，台詞可能如以下「你是一個好人，不是你的問題，我想我們不適合。」在英文中，可用「in the friendzone」來表達「發好人卡」的意思，字面上的意思就是在「朋友圈內」，維持朋友關係，但兩人的關係就是好朋友，沒有進一步發展成為戀人。「friendzone」也可以當作動詞，可以說「She friend-zoned me.」或是「She put me into the friend-zone.」

MP3 040

「發好人卡」means turn down someone nicely by their crash and in English, it is「in the friend-zone」. In Chinese, when people want to turn down a romantic pursuit from someone else, they may start the conversation by saying things along the line of "You're a good person, but…" to use a euphemistic way of saying "No". To make the one being turn down feel not too bad, people will say "You are a good person, not your problem; I think we are not right for each other." That's how the term comes into use. In English, "in the friend-zone" means the situation in which one of a friendship wishes to move into a romantic relationship, while the other does not. It can be used as verb, such as "She friend-zones me." or "She put me into the friend-zone."

※發信站：「鄉民這樣說」實業坊(ptt.cc) 來自 140.115.208.44
※文章網址：https://www.ptt.cc/bbs/PttNewhand/M.1452581219.A.FAF.

→ **Stephanie77:** How's the date with Mike last night? I think you guys are **perfect for each other**.

昨晚與邁可的約會如何呀？我認為你們很速配耶。

推 **Kim101:** I thought so, too. But after a couple glasses of wine, his **behaviors** would quickly turn **out of control**. He even **vomited** on the restaurant floor. That's so embarrassing.

我本來也這麼覺得，但在幾杯黃湯下肚後，他整個就失控了，他甚至還吐在餐廳地板上，好丟臉啊。

→ **Stephanie77:** Oh that's too bad. So what are you gonna do with him?

真是太糟了，那你之後與他要怎麼樣呢？

推 **Kim101:** I think I'm gonna just keep him in the friendzone. I still adore him as a friend, but maybe not a good **candidate** for potential husband, you know.

我想我會發他好人卡，但我還是很珍惜我們的友情，但他或許不是未來老公的料，你說是吧？

單字加油站

單字	詞性	中譯
1. perfect for each other		天生一對、很速配
2. behavior	n.	行為、舉止
3. out of control		失控
4. vomit	v.	嘔吐
5. candidate	n.	候選人、應試者

倍斯特實業坊〉看版 BESTBOOK_Unit 2-19 自婊

作者 鄉民英文原來是醬！Internet Slang on PTT

標題 「自婊」 Mock yourself

「婊」是一個動詞，指的是用一則評論和玩笑使人難堪。「自婊」指的是開自己玩笑，吐槽自己，而這些評論或玩笑可能是有意的，也可能是無意、不小心的，一種嘲諷自己的行為。大多是自己承認自己的缺點或是講自己的糗事，變成一種好笑的行為。在英文中，與「自婊」意思相近的用詞，可用片語「make self-deprecating comments / jokes」,或是比較一般的用法是 “make fun of self.”「嘲笑自己」。

MP3 041

「婊」is a verb to make comments or make jokes to embarrass others.「自婊」means someone makes fun of themselves accidentally or on purpose and is called “mocking themselves”. Most of “mock yourself” are admitting your disadvantages or share with others about your mistakes, which makes the situation funny. But「自婊」is not an very positive word. The term “mock yourself” in Chinese means you make comments or jokes which embarrass yourself either on purpose or accidentally. In English, “make self-deprecating comments/jokes” carries the same meaning or in a common saying “make fun of self.”

※發信站：「鄉民這樣說」實業坊(ptt.cc) 來自 140.115.208.44
※文章網址：https://www.ptt.cc/bbs/PttNewhand/M.1452581219.A.FAF.

→ **JackChen:** I love the **talk show** host's style of hosting. She likes to make self-deprecating jokes that are just **hilarious**.
我很喜歡那位脫口秀主持人的主持風格，她常常喜歡「自婊」，開許多很好笑的笑話。

推 **Monica151:** You're totally right. And because of this style, you can see that her guests on the show feel very **comfortable** with her. I wish I can host like her on my **campus** radio show.
你說得沒錯，也因為這種風格，她節目上的來賓都感到很自在，我希望我也能像她一樣地來主持我的校園廣播節目。

→ **JackChen:** Don't be too self-critical of yourself. I always enjoy listening to your program.
別對自己太苛刻、「自婊」了，我很喜歡聽妳的廣播節目。

推 **Monica151:** Well, thank you for the kind **compliment**!
哇，真是謝謝你的讚美！

單字加油站

單字	詞性	中譯
1. talk show		脫口秀
2. hilarious	n.	好笑的
3. comfortable	adj.	舒適的、自在的
4. campus	v.	校園
5. compliment	n.	稱讚、讚美

倍斯特實業坊〉 看版 BESTBOOK_Unit 2-20 冏

作者 鄉民英文原來是醬！Internet Slang on PTT

標題 「冏」Awkward、I'm Speechless.

這一個詞是表達尷尬或是無言的感受，當某一個人身處令他感到奇怪又尷尬的情境，或是網路上的對話或交談讓他們感到不知如何回應，可以用「冏」這個特別的字型來回覆，因為這就像自己臉上尷尬表情。在英文中，可用「awkward」或是「I'm speechless.」來表示「冏」的意思。在美國，當現場氣氛變得尷尬時，說一句「awkward」可以化解現場尷尬的氛圍，或是用「I'm speechless.」來傳達出感到無言、無奈或尷尬的感受。這些俏皮的用語可以巧妙地化解尷尬，為尷尬的情境帶點「comic relief」(喜劇效果)，讓原本尷尬的氣氛不再那麼尷尬，稍加緩解一下。

MP3 042

This word is used to express the **sentiment** of awkward and embarrassing feeling or simply speechless. When someone is in an embarrassing situation or a conversation on the Internet that makes them feel **odd** or awkward to respond, they may rely with this Chinese letter「冏」。In English, people use "awkward" and "I am speechless." to show their embarrassment. In the USA, when the situation becomes difficult to **deal with**, people will say "Awkward." in a funny way to make an awkward situation less uncomfortable and **ease** the **tension**. Or they say "I am speechless." to show their helplessness or embarrassment. These slangs can make the awkward conversations more comfortable and less embarrassing cleverly because they bring some comic relief.

※發信站：「鄉民這樣說」實業坊(ptt.cc) 來自 140.115.208.44
※文章網址：https://www.ptt.cc/bbs/PttNewhand/M.1452581219.A.FAF.

→ **Ryan1212:** My date is coming in any second now. We met on gaybar.net and this is our first blind date.

雷恩：我的約會對象隨時都可能進來。我們在 gaybar.net 認識，這是我們第一次相見歡。

推 **Judy332:** Except that you drag me here and pretend to be some stranger sitting at the table next to me.

茱蒂：除了你把我拖來，還假裝是某個坐在鄰座的陌生人之外。

→ **Ryan1212:** Come on! I'm nervous! This is my first date since I broke up with Simon!

雷恩：拜託喔！我很緊張啊！這是我跟賽門分手後第一次約會欸！

推 **Judy:** I know. I'm here for ya.

茱蒂：我知道，所以我來了呀。

→ **Ryan1212:** Oh my, that must be him! He said he'd wear a grey check hat. Wait…that's Simon!

雷恩：天啊，那一定是他！他說他會戴一頂灰色格紋帽。等等…那是賽門啊！

單字加油站

單字	詞性	中譯
1. sentiment	n.	情緒
2. odd	adj.	奇怪的
3. deal with	ph.	處理
4. ease	v.	減輕 減緩
5. tension	n.	緊張，焦慮 焦急

倍斯特實業坊〉 看版 BESTBOOK_Unit 2-21 牛逼

作者 鄉民英文原來是醬！Internet Slang on PTT

標題 「牛逼」「牛」Kick-Ass、Amazing, Something else

「牛逼」源自於大陸，用來讚賞一個人的成就很「強」或是「厲害」。簡單來說，當你覺得某一個人很棒時就可以形容別人「很牛」，一個流行語用來形容一個有成就又成功的人，是目前在中國很常用的一個詞。在英文中，當一個人或是一件事情棒到讓人難以相信時，會用「kick-ass」、「amazing」、「something else」來讚賞這真是太特別了，或是用「amazing」來表示因為某一個人太優秀而感到驚嘆，或當你想讚美某一個真是特別也優秀，你就形容他真的是「something else」。

MP3 043

This term "牛" is originally from China and is used to express **admiration** to others and to **praise** others' **achievement**. In short, this informal term is used when you feel like someone is amazing or brilliant. The slang "cow" in Chinese is recently used to describe someone is with great achievement and successful, and it is a popular and informal **compliment** in China now. In English, "kick-ass", "amazing" and "something else" carry the same meaning. When you are surprised that someone or something is too amazing to be true, then you say "Amazing!" to show your surprise. Or you want to praise someone is so **special** and brilliant, then you say she or he is really "something else".

※發信站：「鄉民這樣說」實業坊(ptt.cc) 來自 140.115.208.44
※文章網址：https://www.ptt.cc/bbs/PttNewhand/M.1452581219.A.FAF.

→ **Judy:** What takes you so long? You're late for an hour!
茱蒂：怎麼這麼慢！你遲到一小時了！

推 **Billy:** I'm sorry, I went to my hairdresser and it took longer than I expected.
比利：對不起，我去剪頭髮，結果花的時間比預料中還久。

→ **Judy:** Yeah, look at your kick-ass hair. I assume it's not cheap either, huh?
茱蒂：瞧瞧你的頭髮，真牛逼。我看也不便宜吧？

推 **Billy:** We don't need to go there. Hey, check it out, I got this new wearable device that shows my daily step and calorie burn.
比利：別提了。看看這個，這是我新買的穿戴式裝置，上頭會顯示每日步數和燃燒的卡路里。

→ **Judy:** Amazing. You are like a shimmering hipster almost!
茱蒂：酷喔，你簡直是個閃閃發光的文青嘛！

單字加油站

單字	詞性	中譯
1. admiration	n.	欣賞
2. praise	v.	讚揚
3. compliment	n.	恭維話
4. special	adj.	特別的
5. achievement	n.	成績

倍斯特實業坊〉 看版 BESTBOOK_Unit 2-22 給力

作者	鄉民英文原來是醬！Internet Slang on PTT
標題	「給力」Gelivable、You can always count on someone or something.

「給力」是用來形容人很可靠，通常只要他或她出馬，事情總能順利完成，稱讚他們很厲害又可靠，所以當交付事情給他們時，不需要擔心事情會失敗，他們一定會如期完成。由於「給力」這個中文字詞的盛行，英文甚至有了「給力」這個中文字詞的音義字「gelivable」。是直接由「給力」的中文音譯而來的，不過一般母語為英文的外國人應該不太熟悉這個字，較常見的用法是「You can always count on someone or something」，是指某人或某一個物品很可靠、很值得信賴。

MP3 044

「給力」this term is used to express that someone is very **reliable**. Once the person comes forward and starts doing something, he or she is usually very **successful** in getting things done. In general, when you use this term to describe someone, you mean you can trust and believe someone works well in the way you **expect** on time. Because of its **popularity**, there comes even a Chinglish “gelivable” , but it is not familiar with English **native** speakers, so there is another popular term of use “You can always count on someone or something.”.

※發信站：「鄉民這樣說」實業坊(ptt.cc) 來自 140.115.208.44
※文章網址：https://www.ptt.cc/bbs/PttNewhand/M.1452581219.A.FAF.

→ **Ryan:** And the coleslaw. I said it needs to be made in advance and sit in the refrigerator for at least four hours.

雷恩：涼拌高麗菜呢？我說要提早做好，至少冷藏四小時。

推 **Billy:** Shattered that cabbage and gave it a good toss with that mayo.

比利：早就把高麗菜切妥妥，跟美乃滋拌好了。

→ **Ryan:** You remember to drain the veggies before it hit the oil?

雷恩：加美乃滋之前有先把蔬菜的水份瀝乾嗎？

→ **Billy:** Nobody likes soggy coleslaw. It's all done. You can try some if you don't trust me.

比利：沒人喜歡濕搭搭的沙拉啦，都搞定了。不相信我的話，試吃看看就知道。

推 **Ryan:** That's so good. I knew I can always count on you, buddy!

雷恩：有夠好吃。老弟，我就知道你給力！

單字加油站

單字	詞性	中譯
1. reliable	adj.	值得信賴的
2. expect	v.	預期
3. successful	adj.	成功的
4. popularity	n.	受歡迎程度
5. native	adj.	本國的

倍斯特實業坊〉 看版 BESTBOOK_Unit 2-23 學霸

作者 鄉民英文原來是醬！Internet Slang on PTT

標題 學霸 A straight-A student

學校裡什麼人都有，而科科拿滿分，能用成績傲視群雄的霸主，當然就是學霸了。「學霸」本來是流行於中國網路論壇的用詞，後來輾轉流行到台灣來，現在儼然已經是台灣和中國日常生活中耳熟能詳的詞彙。與學霸相反的字是「學渣」，意思是對讀書一竅不通，完全不擅長讀書的人。不只亞洲父母重視成績，西方國家其實也會有父母要求孩子當學霸。但是太嚴厲要求孩子當學霸，往往導致當事人陷入對未來的茫然。人生不一定要當學霸，但找到一件讓自己能投入做到好的事，絕對是幸福的。

MP3 045

There are all kinds of students in the school, and those who pass every exam with flying colors, looking down with their top-notch **academic** achievement, are **undoubtedly** “straight-A students”. The use of this Chinese term 「學霸」 came from the forum of mainland China. At first, it was only popular among Chinese netizens. After a while it makes its way in Taiwan, and has now become an everyday word in Taiwanese society. Opposite from straight-A is probably straight-F, which refers to students that are not cut out for the study. However, emphasizing on scores is not a **privilege** of Asian parents. In the Western world, there are also parents who take children’s grades very seriously. The result, nevertheless, is that the more they are being forced to take straight-As, the more they tend to be at a loss of future direction. Being a straight-A student doesn’t **guarantee** a perfect life, but finding something you truly love and are good at is certainly the **happiness** in life.

※發信站：「鄉民這樣說」實業坊(ptt.cc) 來自 140.115.208.44
※文章網址：https://www.ptt.cc/bbs/PttNewhand/M.1452581219.A.FAF.

→ **Judy:** Caroline is such a straight-A student! I wonder if she ever gets on the Internet or going out.

茱蒂：卡洛琳真是超級學霸欸！不知道她有沒有時間上網或出去玩。

推 **Billy:** I know, she's not like us. We are more like straight-F student.

比利：對啊，她跟我們不一樣，我們根本是學渣。

→ **Judy:** I don't understand it. I spent so much time on grammar and still got a C.

茱蒂：我不懂欸，我花好多時間讀文法，還是只拿到 65 分。

推 **Billy:** Not to mention that we both went to 1-on-1 with Mr. White ,and he still nearly failed us.

比利：更別提我們跟懷特先生一對一課後輔導，他還是差點把我們當掉。

→ **Judy:** Forget about it! I'm going out tonight!

茱蒂：管他的！今晚我要出去大玩特玩！

推 **Billy:** Hell yeah! Let's have some fun at the bar!

比利：好耶！我們去酒吧找樂子吧！

單字加油站

單字	詞性	中譯
1. academic	adj.	學術的
2. undoubtedly	adv.	無疑地
3. privilege	n.	特權
4. guarantee	n.	保證
5. happiness	n.	幸福

倍斯特實業坊〉看版 BESTBOOK_Unit 2-24 邊緣人

作者 鄉民英文原來是醬！Internet Slang on PTT

標題 「邊緣人」The outsider

難得放假想出去玩，竟然想不到半個人可以邀？這樣悲情到讓人掬一把同情淚的人，就是現在很流行的「邊緣人」。通常邊緣人會被邊緣化，往往是因為自己害羞內向，不敢主動交朋友。另一種類似邊緣人、但差異極大的類型是刻意被孤立的人。這種人可能很想融入大眾，但卻因特定原因被別人惡意霸凌。跟邊緣人不同的是，被霸凌的人往往很想逃離被霸凌的困境，但邊緣人只要踏出自己的舒適圈，就可以交到朋友了。

MP3 046

It's a long-waited holiday, yet you can't think of one person to hang out with? We can't help but feel pity in situation like this. People in this **dilemma** are what we call an outsider. In general, the reason why a person becomes an **outsider** is because they are too shy to get to know other people. Another kind of person, yet far from being an outsider, is a social outcast. These people are willing to be part of a larger group, yet are bullied and outcast **on purpose** for certain reasons. What is different from an outsider, is that social outcast wants nothing but getting out of the **suppressed** condition, while on the other hand, all that an outsider needs to do is stepping out of their **comfort zone**.

※發信站：「鄉民這樣說」實業坊(ptt.cc) 來自 140.115.208.44
※文章網址：https://www.ptt.cc/bbs/PttNewhand/M.1452581219.A.FAF.

→ **Kim:** You know, I used to be an outsider in class.
金：你知道嗎，以前我在班上是邊緣人。

推 **Billy:** Really? You don't seem like one. I thought you have a million friends!
比利：不會吧？妳看起來一點也不像邊緣人，我還想說妳交友廣闊呢。

→ **Kim:** Yeah, now it's better, but when I was in the middle school, I was shy and couldn't look people in the eyes.
金：對啊，現在好多了，但我國中的時候很害羞，根本不敢看著別人的眼睛。

推 **Billy:** Wow, what a makeover. Now you are completely different.
比利：哇，真是女大十八變，現在妳跟內向完全扯不上邊。

→ **Kim:** I learn to be more outgoing. And yeah, making friends is not as scary as I thought.
金：我有學著外向一點，而且交朋友真的沒有想像中那麼難。

單字加油站

單字	詞性	中譯
1. dilemma	n.	兩難
2. outsider	n.	局外人
3. on purpose		故意
4. suppress	v.	壓抑
5. comfortable zone	n.	舒適圈

倍斯特實業坊〉 看版 BESTBOOK

熱門看板	分類看板

PART 03 → 鄉民經典文化！

倍斯特實業坊〉看版 BESTBOOK_Unit 3-1 幻想文

作者　鄉民英文原來是醬！Internet Slang on PTT

標題　「幻想文」La La Land

當網友認為某一個網友的發文，尤其是在 PTT 上的發文，是捏造出來的文章，就會說這是一篇「幻想文」。因為 PTT 的鄉民大多被預設為沒有女朋友的宅男，「幻想文」常見的主題是女朋友，舉例來說，當有網友 po 文分享或是提到自己的女朋友，女友是正妹的時候，或是情節太誇張，大家就會懷疑內容是幻想、虛構的，有網友就會用「幻想文」來回應，大呼根本沒有 po 文中的女朋友或男朋友。在英文中，可用「La La Land」描述一個不切實際的幻想世界，或是最常見的「fantasy」(幻想、狂想)，有時用「see through rose-colored glasses」指某人活在過於理想的世界，所看到的都是過於美好、不踏實的一面。

MP3 047

There is one kind of posts on the popular forum, PTT in Taiwan ,is largely made up and is called 「幻想文」because of its topic. The topic of these posts is mostly related to girlfriends and the netizens are assumed as the single **nerds**, so obviously the posts are imaginary. Therefore, when they mention a **hot chick** girlfriend or the content of the posts seems too **dramatic** and too **imaginary**, then the netizens will doubt whether it is real or not. They will call it as「幻想文」because there is no such person in the real life. In English, "la la land" means an imaginary place and a place that is **remote** from reality. The most common word about imaginary experience is "fantasy" and "see through rose-colored glasses" is person who is generally optimistic and with cheerful attitude.

※發信站：「鄉民這樣說」實業坊(ptt.cc) 來自 140.115.208.44
※文章網址：https://www.ptt.cc/bbs/PttNewhand/M.1452581219.A.FAF.

→ **Ryan:** Kim always feels that Billy has a crush on her, no matter how many times I tell her that Billy has no interest in her at all.

雷恩：金老是覺得比利煞到她，但我明明告訴她好幾次了，比利對她一點興趣也沒有。

推 **Judy:** That's not a thing. Kim is so good-looking that she thinks no man on earth can resist her.

茱蒂：這早就不是秘密了。金長得那麼美，當然覺得世界上的男人都會拜倒在她的石榴裙下。

→ **Ryan:** I don't think Billy has ever showed any affection towards her though.

雷恩：但我覺得比利從來沒對她特別表現好感啊。

推 **Judy:** Yeah, she probably lives in La-La Land, being her own princess there.

茱蒂：對啊，她可能活在幻想世界吧，當自己世界裡的公主。

→ **Ryan:** Jesus, I wish I had that kind of confidence.

雷恩：老天，真希望我有她那份自信。

單字加油站

單字	詞性	中譯
1. nerd	n.	書呆子
2. hot chick	n.	正妹
3. dramatic	adj.	戲劇化的
4. imaginary	adj	虛構的
5. remote	adj.	遙遠的

倍斯特實業坊〉 看版 BESTBOOK_Unit 3-2 帶風向

作者 鄉民英文原來是醬！Internet Slang on PTT

標題 「帶風向」 Sway Opinions

在 PTT 發文時，前幾個回覆的方向會影響到接下的留言，擁有相似的意見的網友會比較勇於發表意見，持相反意見的就選擇隱藏起來，稱為「風向」。「帶風向」是形容某一些鄉民，特別是黨員或是有特定政治立場的鄉民，喜歡發表一些言論來影響其它人的觀點，讓一些擁有相同觀點的鄉民跟著附和。在英文中，「帶風向」相近的詞語可用「sway opinions」，「sway」這個動詞單字本身是「影響、使動搖」，後面接上「opinions」這個複數名詞單字，也就是要影響、動搖許多人意見的意思。

MP3 048

When you post on PTT, the previous **comments** usually affect the following content of comments; people who have similar opinions will be more willing to leave the comments; while those with **opposite** ideas will choose to stay **silent**, and it is called “wind direction control” in Chinese. Some netizens who are party members or with personal political standpoint will leave many comments in order to further change others' opinions, and some netizens with the same point of view also will stand up to support. In English, you can use “sway opinions”, the word “sway” means moving or **swinging** gently from side to side, and “sway opinions” means to changes the opinions of many people.

※發信站：「鄉民這樣說」實業坊(ptt.cc) 來自 140.115.208.44
※文章網址：https://www.ptt.cc/bbs/PttNewhand/M.1452581219.A.FAF.

→ **Ryan:** Have you seen the news? It is said that once the new mayor swears the oath, he is going to allow free market both in cattle farming and agricultural industry!

雷恩：妳看到新聞沒？聽說新市長只要一上任，就要全面開放畜牧業和農產品市場！

推 **Judy:** No way! If he does that, our products won't stand a chance because Chinese products are so cheap!

茱蒂：不會吧！如果他這麼做，我們的產品肯定會遭殃，因為中國貨太便宜了！

→ **Ryan:** Right? And yet he is pushing! I can't believe our elected authority is selling us out.

雷恩：對吧？但他就是想這麼做！沒想到人民選出來的首長竟然出賣我們。

推 **Judy:** Wait, did you see that on Channel 6? That one only supports certain party! I think this is kind of a media manipulation.

茱蒂：等等，你是看第六台說的嗎？那台只支持特定政黨。我覺得這是某種帶風向。

單字加油站

單字	詞性	中譯
1. comment	n.	評論
2. opposite	adj.	相反的
3. silent	adj.	安靜的
4. support	v.	支持
5. swing	v.	搖擺、搖晃

倍斯特實業坊〉 看版 BESTBOOK_Unit 3-3 打臉

作者	鄉民英文原來是醬！Internet Slang on PTT
標題	打臉 Slap in the face

「打臉」字面上的意義是「打人家的臉」，在台灣「打臉」一詞的意思尤指找出別人錯認的事實，使之丟臉出糗。這一個來源可追溯至周星馳電影中的名台詞「說好不准打臉」。最常見的用法是在網路吵架的鄉民之間，因為很多鄉民特別對一個議題講話很大聲，自信滿滿認為很有道理，有時就會有其他的鄉民拿出一些有力的根據或更專業的知識，直指出那個人的重大事實錯誤或推論謬誤等等，讓那個人很丟臉。在這種情況下，就能說那個人「被打臉了」。

MP3 049

A slap in the face, on the words itself, means to slap someone on the face. In Taiwan, it particularly indicates that one finds out a real fact that puts those who think they are absolutely right **ashamed**. Its origin can be traced back to Stephen Chow's movie, where there is a famous line "We've agreed not to slap on the face!" Quite frequently, we find people speaking **confidently** about certain **issue**s on the Internet, yet after a while other people bring up the **convincing evidences** or professional knowledge that proves the former is wrong. When this happens, one can say "he/she is slapped in the face".

※發信站：「鄉民這樣說」實業坊(ptt.cc) 來自 140.115.208.44

※文章網址：https://www.ptt.cc/bbs/PttNewhand/M.1452581219.A.FAF.

→ **Judy111:** That guy is totally hitting on me. He always brings my coffee with a heart on it and asks me how I'm doing and stuff.

茱蒂：那傢伙煞到我了，每次他都在我的咖啡上畫愛心，還會對我噓寒問暖。

推 **Ryan:** You've got it all wrong, girl. That's called latte art and he is just being polite.

雷恩：妹子，妳完全誤會了。那只不過是拉花，他也只是禮貌性問候。

→ **Judy111:** Let's wait and see. I'm gonna seduce him to come out on me.

茱蒂：等著瞧，我要誘惑他向我告白。

推 **Ryan:** Yeah. You are going to be disappointed.

雷恩：是喔，看來妳要失望了。

(Three days later)（三天後）

→ **Judy111:** I can't believe it! I asked him out last night and he said I'm just a friend!

茱蒂：真不敢相信！昨晚我約他出去，他竟然說我只是個朋友！

推 **Ryan:** I knew it. What a slap in the face right? He is actually into men.

雷恩：我就知道，被打臉了對吧？他其實喜歡的是男人啦。

單字加油站

單字	詞性	中譯
1. ashamed	adj.	難為情的
2. confidently	adv.	自信滿滿地
3. issue	n.	議題
4. convincing	adj.	有說服力的
5. evidence	n.	證據

倍斯特實業坊〉看版 BESTBOOK_Unit 3-4 嘴砲

作者	鄉民英文原來是醬！Internet Slang on PTT
標題	嘴砲 Lip Service

「嘴砲」源自另一個較為粗俗的有關性的用語「打砲」，指的是上床。如果某一個人在床上只用嘴巴服務，那大概沒付出什麼努力，只是說說而已。因此「打嘴砲」的意思是光會把話說得天花亂墜，但卻無法實際執行或沒有意願實行。網路上光說不練的人很多，這種人大多踴躍地在網路上留言、回覆和給意見，但就只是空話。就像是有的政治人物光會開空頭支票，卻不見上任後實行。常聽有人說「又在打嘴砲」，表示對這樣的光說不練感到不耐與憤怒。

MP3 050

Lip service can be **associated with** a rather low-class **sexual** term “to bone someone”, which means to have sex. If one only uses the lips to serve in bed that means he/she is not doing any actual work, just saying. It can be referred to someone who only talks about the **ambitious** goals, yet is unable to **achieve** or not willing to put into practice. There are plenty of these kinds who actively leave comments and give advices online because no matter what they say, they don’t need to take real actions. Or there are politicians giving out beautiful visions, yet do not follow their own words. We hear people say “Lip service again!” to express their impatience and the anger towards their promise-breaking.

※發信站：「鄉民這樣說」實業坊(ptt.cc) 來自 140.115.208.44
※文章網址：https://www.ptt.cc/bbs/PttNewhand/M.1452581219.A.FAF.

→ **Ryan123:** You know what my New Year resolution is?
雷恩：妳知道我的新年新希望是什麼嗎？

推 **Judy:** To achieve the goal that you promise to achieve last year?
茱蒂：完成去年誇口要達到的目標嗎？

→ **Ryan123:** No, girl! Why you always have to be so mean?
雷恩：哪有啊！妹子，為什　妳老愛挖苦我？

推 **Judy:** Let's face it. You said you wanted to lose 10 pounds last year and the year before. How many pounds do you lose now?
茱蒂：面對現實吧，你去年和前年都說要瘦十磅，現在瘦多少了？

→ **Ryan123:** This year will be different. I not only will lose 10 pounds, but will get a new boyfriend for Valentine's Day.
雷恩：今年不一樣好不好，我不僅會瘦十磅，還會在情人節前交到男朋友。

推 **Judy:** Yeah. Keep paying lip service. It's cheap indeed.
茱蒂：對啦，繼續嘴砲沒關係，用說的比較簡單。

單字加油站

單字	詞性	中譯
1. associate with		把…聯想在一起
2. sexual	adj.	性的
3. ambitious	adj.	野心勃勃的
4. achieve	v.	達成
5. consequence	n.	後果

1 其實是諧音來的啦！
2 你這個人的特質吼！
3 鄉民經典文化！
4 網有神回覆！
5 英文鄉民英語

倍斯特實業坊〉看版 BESTBOOK_Unit 3-5 推爆

作者　鄉民英文原來是醬！Internet Slang on PTT

標題　推爆 Bump (to the top)

網路上常說的「推文」或「頂文」是指文章受到網友大力支持，多人留言「推」或「頂」增加人氣。在台灣 PTT 論壇上，文章被推一百次時，標題前面會出現「爆」字，讓網友看出這是一篇被「推爆」的文章。現在「推爆」這一個詞常用來指一件事受到網友大力的支持或認可，造成在網路上瘋傳的現象。這有可能是一件事，或是名人政客的一句話等等。在美國，因推特比較受歡迎，常見人用「轉貼推文」來支持和表示對該文章的贊同，這種轉推次數很多的文章也是一種「推爆」。

MP3 051

When people say “push” or “bump” on the Internet, it means that the subject article has been supported by the netizens, and people comment “push” or “bump” to increase the **popularity** even more. On Taiwanese popular **forum**, PTT, when an article was “bumped” a hundred times, the word “**explosion**” (爆) will appear at the beginning of its title, so the netizens can recognize it as the popular articles. This is what it means to be bump to the top. Now the term is used to describe something is supported or recognized widely and even **go viral** on the Internet. It could be an event or something that **celebrities** or politicians says. In America, Twitter has been one of the biggest social media. Many people show their admiration and agreement of a tweet by re-tweeting it. One can also say that something that has been widely re-tweeted is “bumped to the top”.

※發信站：「鄉民這樣說」實業坊(ptt.cc) 來自 140.115.208.44
※文章網址：https://www.ptt.cc/bbs/PttNewhand/M.1452581219.A.FAF.

→ **Judy262:** Do you know that yesterday a woman got robbed in the parking lot right next to our campus?

茱蒂：你知道昨天有位女性在學校旁邊的停車場被搶嗎？

推 **Ryan:** Are you serious? Did it happen at midnight?

雷恩：不會吧？是在半夜發生的嗎？

→ **Judy262:** No, it was at noon! But two men heard her crying for help and ceased the robber. It was incredible.

茱蒂：不是，是在正中午！但有兩個男人聽到呼救聲，前去把歹徒制伏了。真是不可思議。

推 **Ryan:** Oh, right! I saw it today on news. Their deeds were bumped to the top on the Internet!

雷恩：對喔！今天我有看到新聞報導。他們的善行在網路上被「推爆」了。

→ **Judy262:** We really need more people like them in the society.

茱蒂：這個社會需要更多這種暖男。

單字加油站

單字	詞性	中譯
1. popularity	n.	普及、聲望
2. forum	n.	論壇
3. explosion	n.	爆炸
4. go viral		瘋傳
5. celebrity	n.	名流

倍斯特實業坊〉 看版 BESTBOOK_Unit 3-6 裝熟

作者 鄉民英文原來是醬！Internet Slang on PTT

標題 裝熟 Are we close?

「裝熟」意為明明與某人不熟，卻在言行舉止上表現得與對方很熟、甚至像知心好友一樣。在今日社群媒體氾濫的時代，此現象尤其明顯，因為人們在網路上看著別人的生活，會自以為與對方熟識，實際上忘了只是與對方在生活上毫無交集或交集很少的陌生人。在綜藝節目上，也常看到主持人與來賓「裝熟」的例子，有時反而會讓自己碰一鼻子灰。

MP3 052

If one is not **familiar with** another person, yet in their speaking and behaviors pretend to be their "BFFs", you may say he/she is "pretending to be familiar with someone". This is a particular **phenomenon** especially in today's social-media-filled society because following others online accounts gives us an **illusion** that we know one another well, forgetting the fact that to the opposite party, you are nothing more than a **stranger** living in **parallel** world or a friend with less connections. In the variety shows, this often happens when the hosts try to break the ice with their guests faster, but sometimes they face with their cold shoulders instead.

※發信站：「鄉民這樣說」實業坊(ptt.cc) 來自 140.115.208.44

※文章網址：https://www.ptt.cc/bbs/PttNewhand/M.1452581219.A.FAF.

→ **TV** host: Let's welcome our special guest today, Katie Lee!

電視主持人：讓我們歡迎今天的特別來賓李凱蒂！

推 **Katie:** Hello everybody, I'm so glad to be here.

凱蒂：大家好，很高興來上節目。

→ **TV** host: Katie is one of the most up-and-coming actresses and has been nominated in Oscar Award!

電視主持人：凱蒂是最出色的新銳女演員之一，還已經接受過奧斯卡提名！

推 **Katie:** Thank you. I would say that's a thousand prayers come true.

凱蒂：謝謝，應該是我的祈禱奏效了吧。

→ **TV** host: Recently you were caught to be hanging out with the famous DJ Kevin Harris, and he is definitely smoking hot. Katie, how is it like to have a hot dude like him around?

電視主持人：最近妳被逮到跟知名 DJ 凱文哈里斯走得很近，而他顯然是個高富帥。凱蒂，跟這種帥哥在一起感覺如何？

推 **Katie:** Are we close? Because that is none of your business.

凱蒂：別裝熟好嗎？這不關你的事。

單字加油站

單字	詞性	中譯
1. be familiar with	ph.	對…熟悉
2. phenomenon	n.	現象
3. illusion	n.	假象
4. parallel	adj.	平行的
5. stranger	n.	陌生人

倍斯特實業坊〉 看版 BESTBOOK_Unit 3-7 靠譜

作者	鄉民英文原來是醬！Internet Slang on PTT
標題	靠譜 Reliable

靠譜據傳原本是中國北方的慣用語，後來漸漸在台灣地區流行起來，近幾年來更是四處可見。靠譜字面上的意思是「靠」著「譜」，也就是形容一個人靠得住、可以信賴，可用來形容人或事情。而靠譜的反義詞就是「離譜」，字面上的意思就是「離開譜」，用來形容人或事情令人無法置信或脫序。這個詞彙倒是已經在台灣社會流行數十年之久。

MP3 053

Word 「靠譜」 (kao-pu) is a term originally from the North of China. As time goes by, it becomes more and more popular in the **region** of Taiwan. It is widely-used **especially** these years. Kao-pu on its word means to “lean on the sheet”, indicates that someone or something is **reliable**, trust-worthy and doable. The opposite word for kao-pu is li-pu (離譜), which literally means to leave the sheet. It refers to someone or something that is **unbelievably** awful or out of control. This term, however, has been used quite commonly in Taiwanese society for **decades**.

※發信站：「鄉民這樣說」實業坊(ptt.cc) 來自 140.115.208.44
※文章網址：https://www.ptt.cc/bbs/PttNewhand/M.1452581219.A.FAF.

→ **Rachel:** What kind of boyfriend do you want? You have rejected so many!

雷恩：妳到底想要哪種男友？好多人都被妳拒絕了！

推 **Judy:** Well, all I want is a guy who is reliable. Simple as that.

茱蒂：我只想找一個靠譜的男人，就這麼簡單。

→ **Rachel:** For example?

雷恩：舉例來說？

推 **Judy:** His income cannot be less than two millions per year. And I don't want to live with his parents, so he'd better be an orphan.

茱蒂：他的年收入不能少於兩百萬。而且我不想跟他爸媽住，所以他最好是孤兒。

→ **Rachel:** I mean…that is not simple at all. I think a man who is trust-worthy will put me in the first place, and that's all I ask for.

雷恩：我說啊…這樣一點也不簡單。我認為一個靠譜的男人會把我放在第一位，這樣就夠了。

單字加油站

單字	詞性	中譯
1. region	n.	地區
2. especially	adv.	尤其
3. reliable	adj.	可靠的
4. unbelievably	adv.	難以置信地
5. decade	n.	十年

倍斯特實業坊〉 看版 BESTBOOK_Unit 3-8 洋蔥文

作者 鄉民英文原來是醬！Internet Slang on PTT

標題 洋蔥文、加了洋蔥 What a tearjerker.

洋蔥讓人流淚，那加了洋蔥的文章呢？當然就會賺人熱淚。在台灣，「加了洋蔥」是形容催淚的事物，而「洋蔥文」則是讓人動容落淚的文章。著名的出處如周星馳電影《食神》中，男主角在料理中加入洋蔥而使評審流淚。網路上常流傳各種無厘頭、搞笑的奇人異事，但如果突然出現溫馨感人的事蹟，往往會看見網友在文章底下留言「有洋蔥」，以表示驚訝與深受感動之意。

MP3 054

Onions make people cry. What about **articles** with onions? That will definitely be a "tearjerker". In Taiwan, people say "something that has onion in it" in Chinese, referring stories that make you cry, and "article with onion" (tearjerker) is the article that jerks your tears. This famous quote can be found in Stephen Chow's movie "God of **Cookery**". There, the **leading male** adds onions to the dish, thus bursts the tears out of the judges' eyes. On the Internet, it's easy to find **weird** stories, posts and videos that make you laugh. Nevertheless, if there's suddenly one that moves your heart, it is common to see people comment below "There's onion in it." to express their **pleasant** surprise.

※發信站：「鄉民這樣說」實業坊(ptt.cc) 來自 140.115.208.44

※文章網址：https://www.ptt.cc/bbs/PttNewhand/M.1452581219.A.FAF.

→ **Ryan:** You know, there is a weird grandma who travels with a real-sized human plaque with her.

雷恩：妳知道嗎？有個怪阿嬤帶了真人尺寸的人形立牌到處旅行耶。

推 **Judy:** That's creepy, isn't it? Why would she do that?

茱蒂：那不是很詭異嗎？她為什麼要那麼做？

→ **Ryan:** The fun thing is, she not only travels everywhere with it, but checks in and has photo with it wherever they go!

雷恩：更怪的是她不只帶它趴趴走，還到處打卡合照！

推 **Judy:** She must really like that plaque.

茱蒂：她肯定很喜歡那塊立牌。

→ **Ryan:** Turns out that's a plague of her husband that recently passed away. She was doing that in remembrance of him.

雷恩：後來我才知道，原來那是她最近過世的老公的人形立牌。她這麼做是為了重溫以前跟老公的美好回憶。

推 **Judy:** Oh my gosh…what a tearjerker.

茱蒂：天哪…有洋蔥。

單字加油站

單字	詞性	中譯
1. article	n.	文章
2. cookery	n.	廚藝
3. leading male	n.	男主角
4. weird	adj.	荒誕的
5. pleasant	adj.	令人愉快的

作者 鄉民英文原來是醬！Internet Slang on PTT

標題 廢文 Shitpost

就如字面上所說，「廢文」是指完全沒有建設性、毫無意義的發文，大多是為了在論壇上衝文章數而發表。在社群媒體為主流的現代，不少人也會為了排遣無聊或純粹讓別人注意到自己，而在網路上張貼毫無意義的貼文。在網路平台上，如果因為懶得查資料而直接貼文詢問大家，容易被網友譏諷為「發廢文」，例如詢問服裝搭配、天氣和抱怨等，因為鄉民覺得主題太無聊了，往往令人提不起興致回應。

MP3 055

Shitpost, quite literally, means totally non-**constructive** and **meaningless** posts, usually for the purpose of personal article count on the forum. Today, with social media leading the **mainstream**, many people have shitposts on their pages just to kill time or to draw other people's attention. On online forum, if one asks questions out of total **laziness**, such as the weather, **recommendations** for outfits or the complaints could be mocked by the netizens as shit-posts as well, since these kinds of questions don't appear to be interesting for anyone.

※發信站：「鄉民這樣說」實業坊(ptt.cc) 來自 140.115.208.44

※文章網址：https://www.ptt.cc/bbs/PttNewhand/M.1452581219.A.FAF.

→ **Judy:** I saw you post on Instagram today. What is it with a piece of soup and a toothbrush?

茱蒂：我看到今天你在 IG 上的貼文，一塊肥皂和一支牙刷是什麼意思？

推 **Ryan:** They are just some random photos.

雷恩：只是隨便拍的。

→ **Judy:** And you wrote "so lonely" below it. I mean, who are you trying to seduce?

茱蒂：你還在下面寫說「好寂寞」。拜託喔，你是想勾引誰？

推 **Ryan:** I'm not seducing anyone! Just don't want people to forget about me.

雷恩：我哪有想勾引誰！只是刷個存在感而已。

→ **Judy:** Dude, instead of having shit-post, you should really work on your assignment. It didn't look good last time.

茱蒂：老兄，與其發廢文，不如用心寫作業。上次你的成績可不太好看。

單字加油站

單字	詞性	中譯
1. constructive	adj.	建設性的
2. meaningless	adj.	毫無意義的
3. mainstream	n.	主流
4. laziness	n.	懶惰
5. recommendation	n.	推薦

倍斯特實業坊〉看版 BESTBOOK_Unit 3-10 正義魔人	
作者	鄉民英文原來是醬！Internet Slang on PTT
標題	正義魔人 SJW

社會正義戰士（或稱正義魔人）原是中性或正面名詞，用以指稱投身社會正義運動的人。現在衍生為硬把自己的道德、正義標準套在別人身上，而且標準還頗高的網友，只要別人不達標，就猛烈攻擊對方的人。後來這個字出現在美國社交軟體推特(Twitter)上時，意思卻已經從最初的正面轉為負面貶義。現在的正義魔人常用來諷刺主觀認定某一種價值，卻沒有任何深層信念，用虛偽的正義討論或行動主義提高個人地位的人。當在網路上討論某一些社會議題，如女性主義、民權、多元文化、身份認同的議題上，常見有人高呼「正義」口號後，反遭網友譏諷為「正義魔人」。

MP3 056

Social Justice Warrior (SJW) was originally a **neutral** or a positive term, indicating those who fight for justice **campaign**. However, when this term appeared on Twitter, its meaning **switched** from positive to negative. Now “SJW” are often used to describe those who have certain subjective **mindset**, yet without any **profound** beliefs. They fake on having justice-related discussion or pretend to be an activist, with the goal to uplift their personal status. When the netizens discuss on the issues of feminism, civil rights, multiculturalism, identification and so on, we see quite frequently that after someone talks about “justice”, others would fight back by accusing them being “SJW”.

※發信站：「鄉民這樣說」實業坊(ptt.cc) 來自 140.115.208.44
※文章網址：https://www.ptt.cc/bbs/PttNewhand/M.1452581219.A.FAF.

→ **Ryan:** Mia doesn't support marriage equality. She says that a family should consist of one man and one woman.

雷恩：米亞不支持婚姻平權。她說家庭應該由一男一女組成。

推 **Judy:** She is so old-school. I'm not surprised though.

茱蒂：她真是食古不化，但我也不驚訝就是了。

→ **Ryan:** When I say I'd vote for it, she smacked me and asks me if I'm gay!

雷恩：我說我會投婚姻平權一票，她竟然打我一巴掌，還問我是不是同志！

推 **Judy:** What? How dare she? Who does she think she is?

茱蒂：什麼？好大的膽子！她以為自己是誰啊？

→ **Ryan:** I know. But I didn't say anything and she gave me a lecture about how gay people would cripple the society.

雷恩：我知道，但我什麼都沒說。她跟我說教，說同志會害整個社會垮掉。

推 **Judy:** She is such a "SJW".

茱蒂：真是不折不扣的正義魔人。

單字加油站

單字	詞性	中譯
1. neutral	adj.	中性、中立的
2. campaign	n.	運動；活動
3. switch	v.	切換
4. mindset	n.	心態
5. profound	adj.	深刻的

倍斯特實業坊〉看版 BESTBOOK_Unit 3-11 撥接魂

作者	鄉民英文原來是醬！Internet Slang on PTT
標題	撥接魂 From Stone Age

ADSL 技術出現以前，撥接連線是上網的唯一方法，在台灣，網友常用「撥接魂」這種說法來形容某一人接收資訊的速度太慢，以致跟不上時事。另有一種說法「飛鴿傳書」，也是強調一個人的接收資訊的速度很慢，甚至連撥接連線都談不上。在英文裡，類似的用法有「來自石器時代」，形容某一個人像原始人一樣不諳現代科技產品，或不了解最近的最新流行趨勢。舉例來說，如果有人對最近發燒話題一問三不知，就可以問他：「你來自石器時代嗎？」

MP3 057

Before **broadband** technology appears, dial-up Internet access was the only way to connect to the Internet. In Taiwan, the **netizens** use the term “the soul of the dial-up”, indicating that someone who receives the information so slowly that they couldn’t follow up what’s going on now. There’s also another saying, “mail by pigeon”, to further **emphasize** that one’s information doesn’t even meet up to the dial-up **standard**. In English, there’s a similar saying “from Stone Age”. It is used to describe that someone is not familiar with modern technologies or not **in the know** about the latest recent news. For example, if someone has no idea about the most trending topics, one may ask: “Are you from Stone Age?”

※發信站：「鄉民這樣說」實業坊(ptt.cc) 來自 140.115.208.44
※文章網址：https://www.ptt.cc/bbs/PttNewhand/M.1452581219.A.FAF.

→ **Ryan:** What are you doing? You're cooking up a storm in the kitchen.

雷恩：妳在做什麼？我看妳在廚房忙進忙出。

推 **Judy:** Rolling out pasta by hand.

茱蒂：我在用手揉義大利麵團。

→ **Ryan:** Why don't you use Kitchen Aid? There's pasta maker attached to it.

雷恩：妳怎麼不用攪拌機？可以把義大利麵機接上去。

推 **Judy:** Is there? I have no idea. I don't even use my Kitchen Aid. It's still in my cupboard.

茱蒂：是喔？我都不知道。我還沒用過攪拌機，還放在廚櫃裡呢。

→ **Ryan:** Are you from Stone Age? Nobody rolls out pasta by hand now!

雷恩：妳是原始人喔？現在沒人用手揉麵團了啦！

單字加油站

單字	詞性	中譯
1. broadband	n.	寬頻
2. netizen	n.	網友
3. emphasize	v.	強調
4. standard	n.	標準
5. in the know	ph.	知情的

倍斯特實業坊〉 看版 BESTBOOK_Unit 3-12 系

作者 鄉民英文原來是醬！Internet Slang on PTT

標題 ....系 Are you an expert (or what)?

常見台灣網友說「你 XX 系？」，其用意為駁斥他人並非該領域專家，卻想不懂裝懂，頗有調侃、要對方閉嘴的意思。這種用法的由來是某一個知名藝人在網路上發表個人言論，結果引來網友反駁訕笑，該藝人反問對方「你是否為該領域專家嗎？否則就請別發表高見。」後來許多人引用這一個藝人的發言諷刺他人，但現在更將這一個詞用來指某一個人的確是專家的意思，在英文中，可直接用「你是專家嗎？」以激將法表明自己不想聽取對方的「高見」。

MP3 058

In Taiwan, there's an online slang, "Are you from XXX department?" The sentence is meant to argue that the speaker is no way close to be the **expert** of that field, yet wants to **show off** their knowledge about something. One who says this **aims to** tell the opposite party to watch their tongue. The origin of the slang begins with a Taiwanese celebrity's post on Facebook. He posted his personal opinion on his public Facebook page, which be teased by the netizens. He soon fought back with this **argument**: "Are you major in that department? Or you wouldn't know better." After that it becomes a hit now, many people quote this sentence to **make fun of** others. However, recently it appears that this slang is used to applause someone for being real expert. In English, one could simply ask: "Are you an expert or what?" to directly point out that he/she has no interest in listening to "your suggestions".

※發信站：「鄉民這樣說」實業坊(ptt.cc) 來自 140.115.208.44
※文章網址：https://www.ptt.cc/bbs/PttNewhand/M.1452581219.A.FAF.

→ **Ryan:** IT guys are coming back to Taiwan, thanks to America's tax policy towards Chinese imports! Finally, the future of Taiwan is brightened up!

雷恩：多虧美國對中國進口商品徵收關稅，IT 人才要回流台灣了！台灣的未來終於有希望了！

推 **Judy:** Stop making me laugh. Look at the environment now. Who would give up good salary and stuck in this little island?

茱蒂：別惹我發笑了，看看現在的環境，誰會願意放棄高薪，回來困守這座小島？

→ **Ryan:** You are just being negative. I knew this day would come. In your face, China!

雷恩：妳太悲觀了，我早就知道這天會到來。中國，知道厲害了吧！

推 **Judy:** Are you major in economy or what? I'm so sick of your "expertise"!

茱蒂：你是經濟系的嗎？真受不了你的「高見」。

單字加油站

單字	詞性	中譯
1. expert	n.	專家
2. show off	ph.	炫耀、賣弄
3. aim to		旨在
4. argument	n.	理由、論點
5. make fun of	ph.	取笑

倍斯特實業坊〉看版 BESTBOOK_Unit 3-13 打醬油

作者 鄉民英文原來是醬！Internet Slang on PTT

標題 打醬油 I am just passing by./None of one's business

「打醬油」的用法源於中國，原本是某家電視台記者隨機採訪民眾對某一則時事新聞的看法，豈料該名受訪民眾竟從容答道：「我不知道，關我什麼事，我是來買醬油的」。後來「打醬油」一詞便被廣泛用在形容對公眾事務不關心，或事情超出自己能力範圍，因此無能為力。後來更引申為「路人」、電視劇中的跑龍套角色，或是不認真做事、只想打迷糊仗的人。在英文中，可以說「那不關我的事！」或「他只是路過」來指「打醬油」事不關己的意思。

MP3 059

The saying "getting some soy sauce" originates in China. It all starts from a **reporter** asked one passerby's opinions on certain piece of news. To the reporter's surprise, the guy **calmly** answered: " I don't know. I'm just passing by. I'm on my way to buy soy sauce." After that, "beating the soy sauce" is widely used to indicate that one's **indifference** towards public affairs, or that the issue is out of one's hand that he/she can't do anything about it. Nowadays, this saying has **evolved** to be a **synonym** of a random guy, a small role in a show, or a carless player who has no intention to pour his heart out. In English, one can say "That's none of my business." or "He is just passing by." to express the unconcern of one's own.

※發信站：「鄉民這樣說」實業坊(ptt.cc) 來自 140.115.208.44
※文章網址：https://www.ptt.cc/bbs/PttNewhand/M.1452581219.A.FAF.

→ **Ryan:** I can't put up with the new part-time girl anymore. She is always playing with her phone and shows zero passion to work.

雷恩：我受不了新來的工讀生了，她沒事就在滑手機，對工作一點熱情都沒有。

推 **Judy:** Didn't you tell her to be serious about the job? She is a rookie; she'd listen to you, wouldn't she?

茱蒂：你沒叫她認真一點嗎？她是菜鳥，應該會聽你的吧？

→ **Ryan:** I've already told her several times, but I'm not the boss, she wouldn't listen.

雷恩：我講過好幾遍了，但我不是老闆，她根本不甩我。

推 **Judy:** So awful to have this kind of co-worker. She does no good to you.

茱蒂：有這種同事真可怕，只會扯別人後腿。

→ **Ryan:** I know. She pretends it's none of her business. That's really a bad attitude.

雷恩：我知道，她根本是來打醬油的，這種態度真不可取。

單字加油站

單字	詞性	中譯
1. reporter	n.	記者
2. calmly	adv.	冷靜、平靜地
3. indifference	n.	冷漠
4. evolve	v.	演變
5. synonym	n.	同義詞

倍斯特實業坊〉看版 BESTBOOK_Unit 3-14 高富帥

作者　鄉民英文原來是醬！Internet Slang on PTT

標題　高富帥 Smoking hot

高富帥原為大陸用語，用來形容男子身材高、有錢、外表俊俏，與中文傳統刻板印象中的三高（學歷高、身材高、收入高）不一樣。「高富帥」常當名詞使用，用來指女孩子的天菜帥哥或夢中情人。在現代社會裡，身材挺拔不一定長的帥，但在女生眼中，「高富帥」帥哥的定義肯定是身高高、又有經濟能力的。在英文中，如果想描述一個男人帥到讓你「凍未條」，可以說他「帥到冒煙」(smoking hot)，言下之意就是讓人很想直接撲上去了！

MP3 060

The term Gaofushuai (高富帥) originally comes from China. It refers to men that are tall, **wealthy** and handsome. It is slightly different from the **traditional** “three-high” **stereotype** in Chinese society, which refers to high education, tall and good income. Gaofushuai is usually used as a noun, indicating girls’ prince charming or Mr. Right. In modern society, the man who is tall is not always a hottie. However, a good-looking guy in women’s eyes is usually tall and full of cash. If you want to describe a man that’s too hot to **resist**, you can say he is “smoking hot”, which means that you can’t wait to date him!

※發信站：「鄉民這樣說」實業坊(ptt.cc) 來自 140.115.208.44
※文章網址：https://www.ptt.cc/bbs/PttNewhand/M.1452581219.A.FAF.

→ **Ryan:** Have you lost the ability to date a guy? You have been single for like eight months!

雷恩：妳是不是失去跟人約會的能力了？都已經單身八個月了！

推 **Judy:** Of course not! I am just waiting for my Mr. Right.

茱蒂：哪有！我只是在等真命天子出現。

→ **Ryan:** You mean a guy who earns two million per year and has no parents? Come on!

雷恩：妳是說年收入兩百萬，而且父母雙亡的人？拜託喔！

推 **Judy:** Don't be so sarcastic. Besides, I am serious about that one.

茱蒂：別講話帶刺。再說，我可是認真的。

→ **Ryan:** What about the guy sitting behind you? He is smoking hot!

雷恩：那個坐在妳後面的人怎麼樣？他簡直帥到掉渣！

推 **Judy:** Oh my…Look at his Burberry jacket. I'm sure he is the guy.

茱蒂：天哪…看看他的大衣，是 Burberry 的。我看就是他了。

單字加油站

單字	詞性	中譯
1. wealthy	adj.	富裕的
2. traditional	adj.	傳統的
3. stereotype	n.	刻板印象
4. guarantee	n.	保證
5. resist	v.	抵抗

作者 鄉民英文原來是醬！Internet Slang on PTT

標題 白富美 White rich beauty

「高富帥」和「白富美」這兩個詞來自中國形容女性擁有好肌膚、富有又美麗。近年來中國經濟起飛，大多形容一群擁有優良條件的中國年輕一代，是一個對應「高富帥」的稱呼，讚美女生擁有良好的條件，類似台灣「人生勝利組」的意思。因為中國人認為「一白遮三醜」，而財富對想過上流社會的人來說無非是必要條件。兼具二者又長得美的女孩，可說是每一個男人的幻想，也是每一個女生的夢想。在英文中，相關單字「uptown girl」指的就是有錢，見多識廣的和成長在富裕環境的千金小姐。

MP3 061

The word **contrary to** “Gaofushuai” is “Baifumei”, which means women that are **fair-skinned**, rich and beautiful. These two words originate from the appearance of rich young generation in China because of the fastest-growing economy of China. There are many Chinese youth with the whole package and “white rich beauty” is a compliment to those young and rich Chinese girls. Chinese consider fair skin as one of the important elements of beauty and wealth is **no doubt** for those who want to live a high-class life a **necessity** to survive. Beautiful women that have both two **qualities** are definitely the princess of every man and the dream of every woman. In English, “uptown girl” is a girl who is rich, sophisticated and grew up in the comforts and wealthy family.

※發信站：「鄉民這樣說」實業坊(ptt.cc) 來自 140.115.208.44
※文章網址：https://www.ptt.cc/bbs/PttNewhand/M.1452581219.A.FAF.

→ **Judy:** I don't think any girl appears on your radar. Is there?

茱蒂：你好像沒有半個看得上眼的女生，對不對？

推 **Billy:** There certainly is. I just appreciate though. Don't mean that I will fall for her.

比利：有啊，但我只是純欣賞，我可不會愛上人家。

→ **Judy:** Haven't you ever thought of being in the relationship?

茱蒂：你沒想過要談戀愛嗎？

推 **Billy:** Love is a complicated thing. I might as well just put the attention on myself.

比利：愛是一件複雜的事。我還不如把注意力放在自己身上就好。

→ **Judy:** Look! It's Valerie! She is so tall, beautiful and drives her sport car. Look at those legs!

茱蒂：看！是薇樂莉！她又高又美又開著她的跑車，看看那雙逆天長腿！

推 **Billy:** I know. She is a white rich beauty.

比利：我知道，她是一個「白富美」。

單字加油站

單字	詞性	中譯
1. contrary to		與…相反
2. fair skinned	adj.	擁有好肌膚的
3. no doubt		不用說
4. necessity	n.	必需品
5. quality	n.	特質

倍斯特實業坊〉看版 BESTBOOK_Unit 3-16 神馬

作者	鄉民英文原來是醬！Internet Slang on PTT
標題	神馬 Nothing matters.

「神馬」是中文「什麼」的諧音，一開始是大陸網友的錯字，這一個詞會在中國流行起來，是因為有網友在文章中提到「神馬都是浮雲」，意思是一切都是浮雲，小事不值得一提，有點打擊過度、死心的味道。神馬就像西方世界的「獨角獸」，用來形容虛無縹緲的事物，但獨角獸用來形容太過美好、不切實際的事物，「神馬」則有遁入佛門的出世之感。英文可以用「Nothing matters.」「什麼都無所謂」或「我才不在乎」來表示「神馬」的神仙之氣。

MP3 062

"Magic horse" sounds very much like "What" in Chinese. It was a **typo** from the Chinese netizens in the first place. This term became a hit after a guy posted an article online, saying that "Magic horse is nothing but clouds." What he originally meant was that nothing mattered; it is what it is. He couldn't do anything about it at that point (to change it). "Magic horse" **resembles** to "unicorn" in the western world in some way. They both deliver an **unrealistic** feeling, only that the unicorn **represents** something that's too good to be true, and magic horse is full of Buddhism spirit that is not **distracted** by the outer world. One can simply say "nothing matters" or "I don't care a bit." to express that godly sense of "magic horse".

※發信站：「鄉民這樣說」實業坊(ptt.cc) 來自 140.115.208.44

※文章網址：https://www.ptt.cc/bbs/PttNewhand/M.1452581219.A.FAF.

→ **Billy:** You know, Valerie actually invited me to her room once.

比利：妳知道嗎，其實薇樂莉邀我去過她房間。

推 **Judy:** Really? You must be stoked! She is your dream girl, isn't she?

茱蒂：是喔？你一定樂歪了！她是你的女神，不是嗎？

→ **Billy:** Just calm down and let me tell you. At first, I was excited. But when I entered into her room, it was done.

比利：冷靜點聽我說。剛開始我很興奮，但一進到房間，我就知道結束了。

推 **Judy:** What happened?

茱蒂：怎麼會這樣？

→ **Billy:** Her room is stinky. It smells like a mix of dirty clothes, perfume and the spoiled food!

比利：她的房間臭死了。那味道就像髒衣服、香水和壞掉的食物混雜在一起！

推 **Judy:** As beautiful as she looks, beauty is just skin deep. Nothing matters, bro.

茱蒂：她外表雖美，但美麗是膚淺的。老兄，神馬都是浮雲啦。

單字加油站

單字	詞性	中譯
1. typo	n.	錯別字
2. resemble	v.	與…相似
3. unrealistic	adj.	不切實際的
4. represent	v.	代表
5. distract	v.	打擾

倍斯特實業坊〉看版 BESTBOOK_Unit 3-17 搶頭香

作者　鄉民英文原來是醬！Internet Slang on PTT

標題　「搶頭香」put the first incense stick in Chinese New Year

「搶頭香」是用來形容每年農曆新年各廟宇眾信徒搶插第一炷香的景像，以求全年神明的保佑。現在鄉民們引用這個字詞來形容鄉民在 PTT 上搶到第一個回覆的機會。英文中，歷史上記載了 1849 年發生的「Gold Rush」(淘金潮)，當時也有類似的蜂擁而至的景現，而當時的作法是人們在金礦四周的土地上搶著敲進木樁，以標示為自己的土地，再向政府遞交申請，取得土地權，這一段歷史上的行為被稱作「stake out a claim」來重現當時的活動和遊戲規則，當時淘金熱潮的景現，也是大家騎著馬匹，等著槍鳴後向前衝、敲木樁，都有大家搶第一，佔地盤，先搶先贏的感覺。

MP3 063

This term「搶頭香」 originally describes the scene where during the **Lunar New Year,** pious **worshippers** trying to stick the first **incense stick** at the **temples** in pursuit of year-round protection from the **deities** in Asian world. **People in** Taiwanese believe that the first one with the first incense stick at the temples can have super bless from the God, so everyone tries hard to be the first one among thousands of worshippers the temples in Chinese New Year. Maybe in order to win the best luck, when the netziens see one good post on the forum, then they all want to leave the first comment. In Gold Rush in 1849, people “stake out a claim”, to mark with posts a piece of land belonging to the government that they claim for themselves. Everyone wants to claim a land for themselves when they first discover a land. It is like the netizens stake out a claim of their finding of the good posts on the forum. In addition, now it becomes a common term in daily life to carry the meaning of “first come, first served”. (先搶先贏)

※發信站：「鄉民這樣說」實業坊(ptt.cc) 來自 140.115.208.44
※文章網址：https://www.ptt.cc/bbs/PttNewhand/M.1452581219.A.FAF.

→ **Billy:** Who made that chocolate cheesecake on the table? It's to die for!

比利：桌上的巧克力乳酪蛋糕是誰做的？好吃得要命！

推 **Judy:** You had it already? I didn't because it's such a beautiful thing to watch!

茱蒂：你已經吃過了？我還不敢吃，因為實在太美了！

→ **Billy:** I just had one piece. There's only three pieces left on the table though.

比利：我只吃了一塊，不過桌上也只剩三塊了。

推 **Judy:** What—I can't believe it! It must be Ryan, he loves chocolate everything.

茱蒂：不會吧？真不敢相信！鐵定是雷恩，他愛死一切巧克力製品了。

單字加油站

單字	詞性	中譯
1. worshippers	n.	信徒
2. deity	n.	神祇
3. incense stick	n.	香(尤其在宗教儀式上焚燒的)
4. temple	n.	廟
5. Lunar New Year	n.	中國農曆新年

倍斯特實業坊〉 看版 BESTBOOK_Unit 3-18 懶人包

作者 鄉民英文原來是醬！Internet Slang on PTT

標題 懶人包 “The lazy package” “For dummies”

在中文中，「懶人包」字面上就是將一個嚴肅且複雜的社會議題或是新聞整理地簡單清楚，讓一般人更容易了解它。就如字面解釋，「懶人包」是沒那麼聰明的人也能看懂的文章，他們不需要持續追蹤，或是花時間研究這個議題。由於網路論壇百家爭鳴，網路論壇版面常常一團混亂。許多討論對話具有時效性，可能幾小時後就被淹沒在長長的討論串中，若不密切注意網友的討論，常常讓後來瀏覽的網友看得一頭霧水，這就是為什麼開始有熱心網友開始製作懶人包，在英文中，“For Dummies” 有類似的意思，但它其實是一系列給各種不同領域新手的指南手冊。現在懶人包通稱組織明確、時序分明的整理型文章，在有限的篇幅內解釋複雜的社會議題。

MP3 064

In Chinese, “the lazy package” literally means a post about a serious and complicated social issue or news organized well to make it simple for people to understand. Just like the word itself, “the lazy package” is the easy tasks even for not-so-**intellectual** people and lazy people, and then they don’t need to keep following up or spend time studying the issues. Since everybody can post freely on the Internet, the online forums are usually chaotic. Besides, many discussions there are time-limited because they may be soon covered by thousands of the comments in just few hours after it appeared in the first place. If one doesn’t keep paying attention carefully, he/she may not be able to catch up. The warmhearted netizens start creating **packages**. In English, “For Dummies” carries the same meaning, but it is a series of instructional books which are intended to present the easy guides for someone new to the certain topics. Now, “For Dummies” are well-organized and rewritten in clear **sequence** online texts and is able to explain complicated issues and news in a short article,

※發信站：「鄉民這樣說」實業坊(ptt.cc) 來自 140.115.208.44
※文章網址：https://www.ptt.cc/bbs/PttNewhand/M.1452581219.A.FAF.

→ **Judy:** My computer shut down again! I can't take it anymore. I'm gonna buy a new one.

茱蒂：我的電腦又當機了！我受不了了，我要買新電腦。

→ **Ryan:** Don't be so emotional! All you have to do is re-installing the Windows system and everything will be just fine.

雷恩：別這麼衝動！妳只要重新安裝 Windows 系統，一切就會沒事了。

→ **Judy:** It's easier to say! Are you gonna help me?

茱蒂：用說的當然簡單！你會幫忙嗎？

→ **Ryan:** Of course. Here's the CD and instructions. Don't forget to backup important data first!

雷恩：當然囉。這是安裝光碟和安裝說明，別忘了先備份重要資料！

→ **Judy:** This is way too complicated! I'm not an IT girl! Don't you have the instructions "For Dummies"?

茱蒂：這太複雜了！我又不擅長資訊類的東西！你就沒有安裝教學懶人包嗎？

單字加油站

單字	詞性	中譯
1. complicated	adj.	複雜的
2. ordinary	adj.	普通的、一般的
3. intellectual	adj.	智力的、聰明的
4. package	n.	包裹
5. sequence	n.	順序

倍斯特實業坊〉 看版 BESTBOOK_Unit 3-19 幫高調

作者 鄉民英文原來是醬！Internet Slang on PTT

標題 「幫高調」Retweet

「幫高調」在 PTT 是一種很流行的用語，是台灣鄉民希望透過按「推」幫助一篇文章得到更多人關注的方式。很多時候「幫高調」的文章是緊急的尋人文、尋物文，或是希望短時間找到影片中的某一個人，熱心的鄉民就透過在回覆「推文」，讓這一篇文章的推文數增加，讓更多人注意到這一篇文章。在英文中，「retweet」有一樣的效果，在美國比較熱門社群軟體 Twitter(推特)上，當美國網民想要讓一則發文散播出去，就透過「RT @user: xxxxx」格式將這個推特貼文回傳下去，只需要幾個 RT 後訊息就能被很多人看到。被「retweet」最多的貼文也代表是最近很夯，很多人討論的貼文，也比較容易引起別人的注意囉！

MP3 065

「幫高調」a popular term in the cyber world and clicking “bump” on the comments is a way Taiwanese netizens hope to **promote** certain articles in order to catch people’s attention. Most of the time, if not always, these「幫高調」articles are either **urgent** missing person poster or object-**hunting** posts. Whenever the author wishes to hunt down someone in a video in a short period of time, the **kind-hearted** netizens would “bump” the article, increasing the number counts so that more people would notice. In English, “retweet” has similar effect. On one of America’s hottest social media Twitter, whenever a user wants to spread out certain posts, they type under the **format** of “RT @user: xxxxx”. They don’t need more than a few RT for more people to see it. Articles being retweeted the most usually are the hottest ones, therefore they can easily catch people’s eyes.

※發信站：「鄉民這樣說」實業坊(ptt.cc) 來自 140.115.208.44
※文章網址：https://www.ptt.cc/bbs/PttNewhand/M.1452581219.A.FAF.

→ **Kim:** The guy ran away after a girl was hit by his car. Her friend got a video and posted online, hoping to find this criminal.

金：那傢伙開車撞倒一個女孩子，結果肇逃。她朋友拍下過程 po 上網，希望能抓到兇手。

推 **Judy:** And then? Did they find him?

茱蒂：結果呢？有找到人嗎？

→ **Kim:** Yeah. The netizens retweeted it so hard and the guy was arrested few hours ago.

金：有啊，鄉民到處「幫高調」，結果那傢伙幾小時前被捕了。

推 **Judy:** Wow. I guess you just can't do anything illegal and wish to get off the hook these days.

茱蒂：天哪，這年頭真的不能做壞事還以為自己逃得掉。

單字加油站

單字	詞性	中譯
1. promote	v.	促進、發揚光大
2. urgent	adj.	緊急的
3. hunt	v.	獵取、搜索
4. kind-hearted	adj.	好心的
5. format	n.	格式

倍斯特實業坊〉看版 BESTBOOK

熱門看板　分類看板

PART

04 → 網友神回覆！

倍斯特實業坊〉看版 BESTBOOK_Unit 4-1 沒圖沒真相

作者　鄉民英文原來是醬！Internet Slang on PTT

標題　沒圖沒真相 Pics or it didn't happen.

這句話常用在有人分享消息時，網友留言要看照片，尤其文章中提到正妹、辣妹時更是如此。在網路上，有照片就等於有真相，因此如果沒有照片為證，似乎就有信口開河的嫌疑。這個概念可以追溯到 2004 年台灣總統大選，當時國民黨喊出「沒驗票沒真相」的口號，後來便逐漸在網路上流行起來並由網友即興創作。

MP3 066

When people share something online, quite commonly we see others saying "Pics or it didn't happen." **urging** them to share photo as well. This happens especially when there are hot **chicks** mentioned in the post. Everyone can post on the Internet, so photos equal to truth on the Internet. If there's no photo attached, it seems that one is just talking **empty**. The concept can also be traced back to 2004. After the presidential election, Kuomintang shouted the **slogan** "Recount the vote for the truth! Or no truth!" Since then, this saying has been widely spread and was captured and improvised by the netizens.

※發信站：「鄉民這樣說」實業坊(ptt.cc) 來自 140.115.208.44
※文章網址：https://www.ptt.cc/bbs/PttNewhand/M.1452581219.A.FAF.

→ **Judy:** I went out with the guy we saw last week at the café.

茱蒂：我跟上次在咖啡廳認識的男生出去約會了。

推 **Ryan:** Oh really? What did you guys do?

雷恩：是喔？你們做了什麼？

→ **Judy:** We went shopping together. He is actually funny and full of humor.

茱蒂：我們一起逛街購物。他其實滿幽默風趣的。

推 **Ryan:** Did you have any special interaction? Did he hold your hands or anything like that?

雷恩：你們有什麼特別的互動嗎？他有牽妳的手之類的嗎？

→ **Judy:** We shared a chocolate parfait. It was a parfait with dark chocolate jelly, chocolate mousse and chocolate ice cream.

茱蒂：我們一起吃巧克力芭菲。那客芭菲有黑巧克力果凍、巧克力慕斯和巧克力冰淇淋。

推 **Ryan:** Pics or it didn't happen!

雷恩：沒圖沒真相！

單字加油站

單字	詞性	中譯
1. urge	v.	慫恿、督促
2. chick	n.	（俚語）女孩子
3. equal to		相當於…
4. empty	adj.	空洞的
5. slogan	n.	標語、口號

倍斯特實業坊〉 看版 BESTBOOK_Unit 4-2 不要問！很恐怖！	
作者	鄉民英文原來是醬！Internet Slang on PTT
標題	不要問很恐怖！ It's scary, don't ask.

「不要問，很恐怖」這句話一開始是出自一位台灣職棒球員口中，一次他在電視上分享童年往事，說到小時候自己曾用「不要問，很恐怖」這句話，讓媽媽不再追問他的去處，因為很搞笑，這句話開始在棒球板瘋狂流行，後來很快就在台灣網路界流行起來。現在當別人想深入了解故事鮮為人知的黑暗面時，常用「不要問，很恐怖」這句話來迴避問題。有趣的是問題的答案不一定是真的恐怖，這只是一個用來逃避回答的逗趣說法而已。

MP3 067

The saying "It's scary, don't ask." originated from a baseball player from Taiwanese baseball league. One time he shared his **childhood** experience on TV, saying that when he was still young, he used to tell his mother "It's scary, don't ask." to **prevent** her from digging where he was going. The saying first went viral on baseball forum because it is hilarious and quickly **took over** the Internet world in Taiwan. Now this **expression** is used when there's a dark side to a story that few people know. If anyone wants to look deeper and discover the dark-side of the story, people may say "It's scary, don't ask." to avoid more questions. Interesting enough, the truth is not always scary; it is just a fun way to stay out of **confrontation**.

※發信站：「鄉民這樣說」實業坊(ptt.cc) 來自 140.115.208.44
※文章網址：https://www.ptt.cc/bbs/PttNewhand/M.1452581219.A.FAF.

推 **Billy:** Last time I went to Valerie's place, it didn't end well.
比利：上次我去薇樂莉她家，結局不是很好。

→ **Judy:** But did you leave immediately?
茱蒂：你有立刻閃人嗎？

推 **Billy:** I couldn't leave because she opened her wardrobe and started asking me what I think about all her outfit!
比利：我沒辦法閃人，因為她打開衣櫃，開始問我對她的穿搭想法！

→ **Judy:** That's terrible! She must have 500 outfits or something.
茱蒂：太可怕了！她應該有五百套衣服吧。

推 **Billy:** Not only that, she's got hats, earrings and all that accessories!
比利：不只如此，她還有帽子和耳環之類的配件！

→ **Judy:** How long did you spend in her place?
茱蒂：你在她家待了多久？

推 **Billy:** It's scary, don't even ask.
比利：不要問，很恐怖。

單字加油站

單字	詞性	中譯
1. childhood	n.	童年
2. prevent	v.	避免、防止
3. take over		接管、佔據
4. expression	n.	用法
5. confrontation	n.	質問、面對

倍斯特實業坊〉看版 BESTBOOK_Unit 4-3 如何一句話惹惱

作者 鄉民英文原來是醬！Internet Slang on PTT

標題 如何一句話惹惱... Get on one's nerve...

「你讀創意設計系？那可以免費幫我設計 logo 嗎？」一竿子打翻一整船的人，這就是「一句話惹怒…」的威力。「一句話惹怒…」曾短暫風靡網路世界，舉凡大學系所、各行各業、居住地區，任何有刻板印象的題目都能成為「一句話惹怒」的經典名句，這句話會受到歡迎，主要是因為戳中人們心中積怨已久的不耐。比如住墾丁就會天天逛墾丁大街？以貌取人最容易摸到聽者的逆鱗。惹惱別人的英文可說「get on one's nerve」（弄到別人的神經），而要別人「別煩我」則可以說「get off my back」（離開我的背！）。

MP3 068

"You major in Art and Design? Can you do me a favor and draw me a logo for free?" Such **assumptions** can always **irritate** people without fail. "How to annoy someone with a one-liner?" once took trend online. No matter its college department, **profession**, region of residence, everything with the stereotype can be the topic of this discussion. "How to annoy..." went viral, however, is because it triggers the anger hidden deep inside of people. Will you shop on Kenting Main Street every day, just because you live there? **Misjudgment** could always rub someone in the wrong way. In English, "get on one's nerve" means to irritate someone. If you want others to leave you alone, try to say "get off my back"!

※發信站：「鄉民這樣說」實業坊(ptt.cc) 來自 140.115.208.44
※文章網址：https://www.ptt.cc/bbs/PttNewhand/M.1452581219.A.FAF.

→ **Kim:** Nice to meet you! I've heard great things about you!

金：幸會！我聽說很多關於妳的好事！

推 **Judy:** Thanks. I don't think Billy's gonna talk good about me though.

茱蒂：謝謝，但我不認為比利會幫我說好話。

→ **Kim:** He's been saying very good things. Trust me. So, you major in English Literature?

金：相信我，他一直在稱讚妳。聽說妳讀外文系？

推 **Judy:** I do. Not the nerdiest department, but certainly not the coolest.

茱蒂：對，不算是最書呆的系，但也不算很強大。

→ **Kim:** You must have a library of world-famous novels and stuff, right? I mean, that's why you study literature. You love books!

金：妳一定有一堆世界名著吧？妳讀文學嘛，一定超愛看書的。

推 **Judy:** God, this girl is getting on my nerve.

茱蒂：老天，這女孩把我惹怒了。

單字加油站

單字	詞性	中譯
1. assumption	n.	假設
2. irritate	v.	激怒
3. profession	n.	職業
4. misjudgment	n.	誤判

倍斯特實業坊〉看版 BESTBOOK_Unit 4-4 認真就輸了

作者 鄉民英文原來是醬！Internet Slang on PTT

標題 **認真就輸了 Why so serious?**

跟曖昧對象 LINE 來 LINE 去，最後才發現對方早就有男友？以為別人要給自己驚喜，結果只是空歡喜一場？人生好難，乾脆輕鬆看待一切，免得自己內傷。中文常說的「認真就輸了」有種無奈、反正改變不了什麼，乾脆放棄的味道，跟對岸用語「神馬都是浮雲」有異曲同工之妙。電影《蝙蝠俠》中，反派角色小丑曾有經典名言「何必這麼認真？」，諷刺蝙蝠俠打擊犯罪的行徑荒唐可笑。既然改變不了環境，那不如改變自己的心態吧！認真就輸啦！

MP3 069

You text a girl back and forth, and only to discover that she already has a boyfriend. You expect others to give you a **surprise**, yet the entire wait turns out to be a thing in your head. Life is hard. Why not joke about it so you don't get hurt? In Chinese, what we usually say "Be no serious or you lose" conveys a sense of helpless. Since there's nothing you can do, giving up may not be a bad **option**. This saying is more or less similar to "everything is just magic horse" in China. In the film The Dark Knight, super **villain** Joker had a famous line "Why so serious?", pointing out that Batman's **determination** against crime is rather **ridiculous**. Well, if you can't alter what's around you, at least you can change what you think. Why so serious?

※發信站：「鄉民這樣說」實業坊(ptt.cc) 來自 140.115.208.44
※文章網址：https://www.ptt.cc/bbs/PttNewhand/M.1452581219.A.FAF.

→ **Kim:** I didn't mean it when I say you are chubby…I mean that's adorable.

金：我不是故意說妳胖…我的意思是，這樣很古錐。

推 **Judy:** Adorable? Puppies are adorable! You don't get to say that just you are tall and skinny!

茱蒂：古錐？狗狗最古錐啦！別以為妳又高又瘦就可以這樣說我！

→ **Kim:** I know I'm perfect. But you've found yourself a place for not being perfect.

金：我知道我很完美，但不完美也有不完美的優點啊。

推 **Judy:** I can't even…You are not the kind of people I can chat with.

茱蒂：我受不了了，跟妳這種人沒辦法溝通。

→ **Kim:** Come on. I like you! You're like my big sister.

金：別這樣嘛，我很喜歡妳耶！妳就像我的姊姊一樣。

推 **Judy:** Yeah. Why so serious? Nothing wrong with being sexy and a little mean.

茱蒂：算了，認真就輸了，反正口無遮攔的正妹也沒什麼不對。

單字加油站

單字	詞性	中譯
1. helpless	adj.	無助的
2. option	n.	選項
3. villain	n.	壞蛋
4. determination	n.	決心
5. ridiculous	adj.	荒唐的

倍斯特實業坊〉看版 BESTBOOK_Unit 4-5 這是什麼巫術！

作者	鄉民英文原來是醬！Internet Slang on PTT
標題	這是什麼巫術！ Jump out of one's skin

乍看之下，「這是什麼巫術！」的含義讓人一頭霧水，其實這句話的典故出自網路，意思是對眼前的景象瞠目結舌、不敢置信。如果有胖胖的女孩子瘦下來後美如天仙，看到前後對照圖的人，就可能大喊「這是什麼巫術！」，同樣的例子也能用在女孩化妝前後、街友大改造之類的，只要讓人大吃一驚，覺得不可思議都可以用。英文「嚇一跳」的用法有很多，例如「jump out of one's skin」（嚇到魂都出竅了）、「knock one's socks off」（嚇到襪子都掉了）之類，讓人驚訝到下巴都掉了，則可以說「make one's jaw drop」。

MP3 070

At first sight, "What is this sorcery?" in Chinese may appear **confusing**. The slang actually comes from the Internet, indicating somebody is utterly shocked and couldn't believe what they see. For instance, if a chubby girl turns out to be a **stunning** beauty after she loses weight, those who see the before-after **comparison** may cry out "what is this sorcery!" Same thing applies to girls before and after make-up or **homeless** guys before and after dressing up. The expression can fit in any situation that is shocking and **unbelievable**. In English, there are quite a few similar sayings, such as "jump out of one's skin" or "knock one's socks off". One can even go further and say "make one's jaw drop".

※發信站：「鄉民這樣說」實業坊(ptt.cc) 來自 140.115.208.44
※文章網址：https://www.ptt.cc/bbs/PttNewhand/M.1452581219.A.FAF.

→ **Kim:** Look at you! You look glamorous! Did you lose weight?

金：瞧瞧，妳簡直美呆了！妳是不是瘦了？

推 **Judy:** Yeah. After you told me I'm "adorable", I've made up my mind to be sexy and lost ten pounds.

茱蒂：對啊，自從妳說我「胖得很古錐」之後，我就決定要變性感，還瘦了十磅呢。

→ **Kim:** That's incredible. But…it must have been only a week. How did you lose weight so fast?

金：太強了吧。但…那應該是一週前的事，妳怎麼瘦得這麼快？

推 **Judy:** You know what? It's not that hard. I don't eat lunch and go swimming regularly.

茱蒂：拜託，一點也不難好不好。我過午不食，而且還定期去游泳。

→ **Kim:** Wow, that makes my jaw drop. I hope you don't get sick.

金：哎唷，這什麼巫術啊。希望妳別把身子搞壞。

單字加油站

單字	詞性	中譯
1. confusing	adj.	令人困惑的
2. stunning	adj.	令人吃驚的
3. comparison	n.	對照
4. homeless	adj.	無家可歸的
5. unbelievable	adj.	令人難以置信的

倍斯特實業坊〉看版 BESTBOOK_Unit 4-6 不就好棒棒

作者　鄉民英文原來是醬！Internet Slang on PTT

標題　**不就好棒棒 Full of shit**

稱讚別人，我們會說「你好棒」，但中文中「好棒棒」是相反的意思，之後就逐漸流行，你遇到有人自認為很厲害、自以為是或炫耀的時候，就用這句話來挖苦那個炫耀個不停的人。有時候為了增強挖苦的感覺，講這句話的人還會加上拍手的動作。如果有人高談闊論，覺得自己不可一世，你聽著卻不以為然，就拍拍手稱讚他「好棒棒」。但講這句話時可要小心，別惹到不該惹的人，免得後果不堪設想！相對的英文用法比較粗俗，「one's full of shit」的意思是某人只會鬼扯，聽他講話根本浪費時間。

MP3 071

When we praise someone, we'd say "you're great", but "you are sooooo great!" in Chinese serves the opposite meaning. It indicates one's disapproval to the subject party and even considers it stupid or idiotic. When someone is showing off and becomes too big for his boots, people say "You are soooo great" for being sarcastic. Sometimes, in order to **enhance** the **ironic** feeling, one may accompany the phrase with the clapping hands. If someone talks like he knows it all, being really confident, yet is annoying to you, you may **compliment** in this sarcastic way. Be careful though when choosing the person to talk to. Some may not take it well. In English, "one's full of shit" **unleashes** ultimate impatience. If one is full of shit, it means that none of his words is credible. Talking to this kind of person is just a waste of time.

※發信站：「鄉民這樣說」實業坊(ptt.cc) 來自 140.115.208.44
※文章網址：https://www.ptt.cc/bbs/PttNewhand/M.1452581219.A.FAF.

→ **Ryan:** I met this guy Johnson online, and he is one of the hottest guys I've ever seen on the dating website.

雷恩：我在網路上認識一個叫強森的傢伙，老天，他是網路上難得一見的天菜！

推 **Judy:** Okay. You've talked about guys a million times, but you still couldn't hook up with any of them!

茱蒂：是喔，你每次都在講男生的事，但到現在還是半個都沒交到。

→ **Ryan:** And I'm gonna have one. It's just really hard to choose among them. There's another Will that works in a technical company, and he is RICH.

雷恩：只是還沒而已，我會交到的，而且很難選啊！我還認識一個叫威爾的工程師，他超多金的。

推 **Judy:** You're so full of shit.

茱蒂：啊不就好棒棒。

→ **Ryan:** What? I'm just finding the perfect match!

雷恩：怎樣啦？我只是想找個完美的對象嘛！

單字加油站

單字	詞性	中譯
1. enhance	v.	加強
2. ironic	adj.	冷嘲熱諷的
3. compliment	n.	讚美
4. unleash	v.	釋放

倍斯特實業坊〉看版 BESTBOOK_Unit 4-7 病魔加油

作者	鄉民英文原來是醬！Internet Slang on PTT
標題	病魔加油 Wish someone the worst

通常別人生病，我們都會祝他早日康復，或是祝福對方一切安好。但如果這個人是你討厭的傢伙，你非但不希望他平安健康，反而希望他「死好」、「趕快死一死」呢？這時候就可以說「病魔加油」，用諷刺的口吻間接唱衰對方。不過就算多火大，在英文中，一般不會當場咒罵別人，會顯得自己很沒教養，因此很少有人會直接這樣說，如果只是跟死黨在背後一起說別人的壞話，可以直接用「fuck XX!」直接了當的表達自己對某一個人或事物的不滿。

MP3 072

Normally, when someone got sick, we'd wish him/her get better soon, or say "We wish them all the best." However, if this guy **unfortunately** does not fall into your "get better soon" list, instead you wish him dead or getting even worst, you may say "I wish you the worst", indicating **indirectly** that you don't want any good things happen to him. In English world, people don't **swear** to other people's face. That way you yourself may seem a little **uncivilized**. So, if you are just **speaking ill of** someone with your buddies, "Fuck XX" would be an easier way to express your anger.

※發信站：「鄉民這樣說」實業坊(ptt.cc) 來自 140.115.208.44
※文章網址：https://www.ptt.cc/bbs/PttNewhand/M.1452581219.A.FAF.

→ **Billy:** Our grammar teacher has day-off today again. The secretary said he's got a fever.

比利：我們的文法老師今天又請假了，秘書說他發燒。

推 **Judy:** I wish him the worst! Finally, justice has served!

茱蒂：病魔加油！正義終於伸張了！

→ **Billy:** You are such a terrible person! What did he do to you that he deserves such evil words?

比利：妳也太狠了吧！他對妳做了什麼嗎？幹嘛這樣詛咒人家？

推 **Judy:** Well, he failed me last semester. I showed up every class and did all the homework, he still failed me!

茱蒂：上學期他把我當了。我每堂課都有去上，每份作業都有交，他還是把我當掉！

→ **Billy:** He is just doing his job. Oh well, maybe he's a little hard to please.

比利：他只是盡責而已。好了，他是真的有點難搞。

單字加油站

單字	詞性	中譯
1. unfortunately	adv.	不幸地
2. indirectly	adv.	間接地
3. swear	v.	罵粗話
4. uncivilized	adj.	野蠻的
5. speak ill of	ph.	說別人壞話

倍斯特實業坊〉 看版 BESTBOOK_Unit 4-8 噓爆

作者	鄉民英文原來是醬！Internet Slang on PTT
標題	噓爆 Suck ass！

相對於廣受大眾認可的「推」，「噓文」也是 PTT 的一個基本功能，「噓」就是網友覺得很遜、爛透了的人事物。通常如果公眾人物發言不當，尤其是政治人物，在政策成效不佳時推卸責任，很容易引起一片噓聲。簡單來說，「被噓爆」則是進一步大家都覺得爛透了。例如：有的脫口秀藝人如果講得太差，也會被台下觀眾丟花生、垃圾之類的東西要他下台，簡單來說，「噓爆」就是很多人對一個人或一件事情表示強烈不認同的意思。

MP3 073

Opposite from “bump”, which means the posts are well-recognized as good or agreed, “OO sucks” means it is lame and unpleasing. In general, when a celebrity gives out an **inappropriate** speech, or a politician sets up a policy that does not deliver ideal results, certain comments or **protests** may arise and the celeb or politician may get **hissed** at. Simply if someone says “sucks ass”, it further indicates that he/she’s **performance** is really bad. For instance, if a talk show host couldn’t bring out the amusement effect that there is supposed to be, the **audience** might throw peanuts or garbage to hiss him off! That is pretty much what it means “suck ass”. In short, “suck ass” means the strong disagreement and dissatisfied of something or someone from a bunch of people.

※發信站：「鄉民這樣說」實業坊(ptt.cc) 來自 140.115.208.44
※文章網址：https://www.ptt.cc/bbs/PttNewhand/M.1452581219.A.FAF.

推 **Judy:** I can't believe the director of the department allows our students go on strike!

茱蒂：真不敢相信我們的系主任竟然同意讓學生參加罷工！

→ **Ryan:** Yeah, those who go on demonstration instead of coming to classes don't even need any proof. They just go.

雷恩：對啊，不來上課去罷工的人還不用證明，想去就去呢。

推 **Judy:** Who knows exactly where they are going? Maybe they are protesting in the KTV!

茱蒂：誰知道他們到底去哪？說不定罷工到 KTV 去哩！

→ **Ryan:** I know. What he did suck ass. I don't agree with it 100%. For me, sitting in front of the President Office is not justifiable.

雷恩：就是說啊，他的做法被噓爆了，我一點也不認同。我可不認為去總統府前面靜坐算什麼正當理由。

推 **Judy:** There will be more and more spoiled brats. That's what's gonna happen.

茱蒂：看來以後屁孩只會越來越多。

單字加油站

單字	詞性	中譯
1. inappropriate	adj.	不恰當的
2. protest	v.	抗議
3. hiss	.	發出噓聲
4. performance	n.	表演、表現
5. audience	n.	觀眾

倍斯特實業坊〉看版 BESTBOOK_Unit 4-9 灑花

作者　鄉民英文原來是醬！Internet Slang on PTT

標題　**灑花 Full of the joys of spring**

當人們開心的時候，總會做出一些傻呼呼的舉動，轉圈、灑花就是其中兩種，像狗狗開心會搖尾巴一樣，一個人開心、露出大大的笑容，灑花 (*￣▽￣)/・☆*”`’*-.,_,.-*’`”*-.,_☆就像旁邊開滿溫暖的小花一樣，讓人如沐春風。有很多英文片語可以形容一個人開心的樣子，「充滿春天的喜樂」(full of the joys of spring) 是其中之一。形容別人就像在春天的花園裡蹦蹦跳跳一樣，一副開心到傻的樣子。如果一個人開心到爆了，可以說他「飛到月球上」(over the moon) 或「置身第七天堂」(in the seventh heaven)，表示開心到不行啦！

MP3 074

People do silly things when they are happy, dancing in circles and **beaming** with energy may be two of them. Like a dog **wag**ing its tail when it is excited. When people are **grinning** from ear to ear, it is like they are in a **blossoming** garden giving out sunshine. There are plenty English phrases for the description of one’s joy, such as “full of the joys of spring”. This phrase sorts of depicts an image of someone jumping, **bouncing** around in a spring garden, where he smiles like a fool. If one’s joy cannot be topped with anything, we may say he/she is “over the moon” or “in seventh heaven”. They all mean that the person is absolutely filled with joy.

※發信站：「鄉民這樣說」實業坊(ptt.cc) 來自 140.115.208.44

※文章網址：https://www.ptt.cc/bbs/PttNewhand/M.1452581219.A.FAF.

推 **Billy:** What's going on? You look like you just won a lottery or something.

比利：怎麼回事？妳看起來好像中樂透一樣。

→ **Kim:** I'm super excited. I got hired at Starbucks and they told me to start tomorrow!

金：我超興奮的！我面試上了星巴克，他們叫我明天上工！

推 **Billy:** Wow, look at the girl bouncing around, full of the joys of spring. I don't think you know what you're getting yourself into.

比利：看看妳，開心到跳來跳去灑花哩！妳大概不知道這份工作有多累吧。

→ **Kim:** Come on, now. I know it's gonna be tough, but I've been dreaming about this FOREVER.

金：別唸了，我知道工作累，但我希望得到這個工作已經很久了。

推 **Billy:** Alright. As long as you are happy with it, fine with me.

比利：好吧，既然妳那麼開心，我也就沒什麼好說的了。

→ **Kim:** Free coffee, here I come!

金：免費咖啡我來啦！

單字加油站

單字	詞性	中譯
1. beam	v.	流露、照射
2. wag	v.	搖擺
3. grin	v.	露齒而笑
4. blossom	v.	開花
5. bounce	v.	彈跳

倍斯特實業坊〉 看版 BESTBOOK_Unit 4-10 跪求

作者 鄉民英文原來是醬！Internet Slang on PTT

標題 跪求 In desperate need of something

跪著求別人施捨，在現實生活中應該只有乞丐會這麼做吧！所謂的跪求其實是要求、尋求幫助的誇張說法，有時候是因為自己怎麼找都找不到答案，跪求別人惠賜資源，有時候只是發懶，想用「伸手牌」招數撿現成的東西使用。不論是哪一種，跪求都表現出很想得到某一種東西的態度，形容一個人超級渴望得到某一個東西，英文可以說「想要 OO 到絕望的地步」(in desperate need of something)，不過中西文化大不同，對不太熟的人不要隨便跪求，對方可能會以為你沒有這個東西會死喔！

MP3 075

Begging someone with knees on the floor, that's probably something only beggars would do in reality. In Taiwan, people like to use "begging for something" as an **exaggeration**, which in fact may not be a **necessity** for them. Some people say so because no matter how hard they try, they cannot find the **resource** they need. Some "beg" just to **take advantage of** others. Either way, the word "beg" delivers a sense of desperation. If one really wants something, one may say "he is in desperate need of OO". However, due to the difference between the East and the West, maybe one should only "beg" to close ones. **Otherwise**, they may think you're gonna die without it!

※發信站：「鄉民這樣說」實業坊(ptt.cc) 來自 140.115.208.44

※文章網址：https://www.ptt.cc/bbs/PttNewhand/M.1452581219.A.FAF.

→ **Judy:** Do you have any idea where I can download this song without vocal?

茱蒂：你知道哪裡能下載這首歌的純音樂版嗎？

推 **Ryan:** Why? Are you making a video or something?

雷恩：幹嘛？妳要做影片啊？

→ **Judy:** Yeah, I really need the music. It's perfect for my video. Come on, I'm in desperate need of a link.

茱蒂：對，我真的很需要這首配樂，跟我的影片超搭的。拜託啦，跪求連結。

推 **Ryan:** You know what? Since you are my bff, I'm gonna make that instrumental version just for you.

雷恩：這樣好了，既然妳是我的好姐妹，我就專程幫妳剪個純音樂版吧。

→ **Judy:** That's so sweet of you!

茱蒂：你也太暖了吧！

推 **Ryan:** Also, you owe me a macchiato grande.

雷恩：還有，妳欠我一杯大的焦糖瑪琪朵。

單字加油站

單字	詞性	中譯
1. exaggeration	n.	誇大
2. necessity	n.	必需品
3. resource	n.	資源
4. take advantage of	ph.	利用
5. otherwise	adv.	否則

倍斯特實業坊〉看版 BESTBOOK_Unit 4-11 不意外

作者	鄉民英文原來是醬！Internet Slang on PTT
標題	不意外 It figures.

如果有人做事老是「凸槌」，卻還把重要的事交給他辦，最後真的搞砸了，旁人就可能搖搖頭說「不意外」。「不意外」帶有強烈的諷刺意味，不僅本來就不看好某一件人事物，真的下場淒慘的話，這句話還有落井下石、潑冷水的感覺和結果如預期一樣一點都不讓人驚訝。其實「不意外」跟「認真就輸了」一樣，都帶有一絲無法改變現實的心灰意冷，和乾脆一笑置之的冷漠感受。這些詞彙廣受歡迎，某一種程度上也反映了人面對社會現實面的無奈。

MP3 076

If one always fucks up on stuff, yet is **assigned** important task, and the result turns out, **to nobody's surprise**, to be a mess. That's when people shake their head and sign "it figures", and the saying expresses a strong sarcastic feeling, indicating that someone or something is expected to go down and fails and the outcome is like peole expected and no surprise. If it does mess up and end up **miserably**, the saying even gives out a mocking effect. In fact, "if figures" (I am not surprised) is just like "Why so serious?" It is the desperation of the reflection to this cruel reality. Since there's nothing we can do, might as well just make fun of it. This term comes in trendy, actually **mirrors** to certain point that people feel helpless in face of the real world.

※發信站：「鄉民這樣說」實業坊(ptt.cc) 來自 140.115.208.44
※文章網址：https://www.ptt.cc/bbs/PttNewhand/M.1452581219.A.FAF.

→ **推** Judy: I think our director of the department to getting replaced. I overheard it today in the office.

茱蒂：我們的系主任好像要換人做了，今天我在辦公室不小心聽到的。

推 Billy: Really? How come?

比利：是喔？為什麼？

→ **推** Judy: I am not sure, but probably because he allows students to go on strike.

茱蒂：我也不知道，可能是因為他讓學生去抗議示威吧。

推 Billy: In that way, if figures. I never approve what he does.

比利：如果是因為那樣，我可不意外。我從來都不認同他的做法。

→ **推** Judy: I know. It's a terrible move. Students are easily manipulated.

茱蒂：我知道，他的做法有夠爛。學生很容易被煽動。

推 Billy: Might as well get another director that has something in his head!

比利：換個有點頭腦的系主任比較好！

單字加油站

單字	詞性	中譯
1. assign	v.	指派
2. miserably	adv.	悲慘地
3. desperation	n.	絕望
4. cruel	adj.	殘忍的
5. mirror	v.	反映

倍斯特實業坊〉看版 BESTBOOK_Unit 4-12 我覺得可以

作者	鄉民英文原來是醬！Internet Slang on PTT
標題	我覺得可以 I dig it.

歌唱節目上紅極一時的「我覺得可以」、「我覺得不行」是當時評審對參賽者表現的評語，如果表現不錯，評審就會說「我覺得可以」，反之則說「覺得不行」。「我覺得可以」，其實就是「我喜歡」、「幹得漂亮」的意思。「我覺得可以」幾乎適用於所有場合，只要覺得某一個東西不錯、還過得去，就可以說「我覺得可以」，類似用法還有「某個東西我喜翻（我愛心某個東西）」和來自臉書的「按讚」。

MP3 077

"I dig it" (I think it's great) "I don't dig it" (I think it's awful) were lines from a Chinese **talent** show where the **judges** reacted to **contestants** using these two famous expressions. If they performed well, the judges compliment them by saying "I dig it." On the other hand, if the performers don't have what it takes to move on, they'd face the "I don't dig it" **sentence**. In other words, "I dig it" equals to "I like it" or "Well done." This term can serve in almost every condition. If someone or an object wins your heart, or simply just doesn't **disgust** you, you might say "I dig it." Similar usages include "I heart it" or "like" from Facebook.

※發信站：「鄉民這樣說」實業坊(ptt.cc) 來自 140.115.208.44
※文章網址：https://www.ptt.cc/bbs/PttNewhand/M.1452581219.A.FAF.

→ **Billy:** What do you think about the café we went last time?

比利：妳覺得我們上次去的咖啡店怎麼樣？

推 **Judy:** I dig it. It was decent. Latte was not impressive but it's okay.

茱蒂：我覺得可以，還 ok 啦，拿鐵不怎麼樣，但還能喝。

→ **Billy:** What do you say we go there again? That place is affordable than most of the other cafés at the same level.

比利：要不要再去一次？那裡比大部分其他同級咖啡店便宜。

推 **Judy:** Sure, why not? Besides, they give you free cookies to go with.

茱蒂：當然好啊，再說，那裡點咖啡還附贈免費小餅乾。

→ **Billy:** Cool, let's go!

比利：讚喔，那我們走吧！

推 **Judy:** Let me just grab my laptop and stuff and we can go.

茱蒂：讓我拿筆電，我們就可以閃人了。

單字加油站

單字	詞性	中譯
1. talent	n.	天份
2. judge	n.	評審
3. contestant	n.	參賽者
4. sentence	n.	判決
5. disgust	v.	使某人反胃

倍斯特實業坊〉 看版 BESTBOOK_Unit 4-13 爆雷

作者 鄉民英文原來是醬！Internet Slang on PTT

標題 爆雷 Spoilers、Spoil

本來只想在上戲院前看看某一部片的評價，卻意外得知劇情發展，就是「爆雷」。「爆雷」形容好像有一顆手榴彈，把別人的期待和喜悅炸得精光，也可以用動詞「雷」使用，例如本來很期待的電影，竟然意外被劇透，或是期待值很高的餐廳讓人失望等等，被狠狠「爆雷」的感覺真不好受。當你在 Instagram 上看到一間超棒的餐廳，實際消費後卻發現難吃得要命。這種感覺實在很糟糕，簡直是賠了夫人又折兵，也算是一種「被雷到」。如果不想雷到別人，記得在文章開頭寫「有劇透！」，別當一個雷人的傢伙吧！

MP3 078

When you just want to check the movie reviews before going to the theater, yet get to know what exactly is going on in the film **unexpectedly**. “Spoilers” is just like a **grenade** that blows up all your expectations, and it can be used as a verb, such as going to a movie got spoiled by spoilers, or a the experience of going highly-**recommended** restaurant turned bad. That’s how it feels to be “spoiled”, which means to destroy or reduce the pleasure of something. Or you discover a great café on Instagram, yet when you go in there, the food is actually **inedible**. That’s another **distressful** experience, penny not very well spent. If you don’t want to be somebody else’s spoiler, don’t forget to add “spoiler alert” at the beginning of an article. That way, you won’t spoil some other’s day.

※發信站：「鄉民這樣說」實業坊(ptt.cc) 來自 140.115.208.44
※文章網址：https://www.ptt.cc/bbs/PttNewhand/M.1452581219.A.FAF.

→ **Ryan:** Have you watched Netflix original series "The Ranch"?

雷恩：妳看過 Netflix 原創影集《牧場家族》嗎？

→ **Kim:** Yeah, season 5 just came out. I watched the whole thing in two days.

金：有啊，第五季剛上線呢。我花兩天就看完了。

→ **Ryan:** Oh great! I've been wondering how Rooster is gonna deal with his girlfriend.

雷恩：太好了！我很好奇公雞跟他女友會怎麼發展。

→ **Kim:** Oh, she is a real pain in the ass. I don't like her one bit. She didn't just hook up with Rooster…

金：她超煩的，我很討厭她，她不只跟公雞有一腿…。

→ **Ryan:** Hey, no spoiler! I want to be surprised.

雷恩：拜託別雷我！我想要有驚喜。

→ **Kim:** Okay, I'll shut up then, or I might just let out!

金：好，那我要閉嘴了，否則可能會不小心講出來！

單字加油站

單字	詞性	中譯
1. unexpectedly	adv.	出乎意料地
2. inedible	adj.	難以下嚥的
3. distressful	adj.	不幸的
4. grenade	n.	手榴彈
5. recommend	v.	推薦

倍斯特實業坊〉 看版 BESTBOOK_Unit 4-14 躺著也中槍

作者 鄉民英文原來是醬！Internet Slang on PTT

標題 躺著也中槍 Get dissed

發射子彈之前通常都會好好瞄準，但如果你只是躺著不動也被波及「中槍」，那就只能自認倒霉了。「躺著也中槍」意思是某一個人什麼也沒做，卻被別人 cue 到，而且通常都是一些負面批評。最愛報導歌手或藝人緋聞的八卦新聞中，以喜歡拿前任男友寫歌的小天后泰勒絲為例，就常常「躺著也中槍」，有人就曾說過因為不想被她寫進歌裡，不考慮跟她交往等等。需要注意的是，中文「躺著也中槍」通常是指沒做什麼但也被波及的含義，但英文「Get dissed」卻帶有說閒話、認為一個人不怎麼樣的負面批評意思居多，很常見但使用上需要注意。

MP3 079

Before shooting a gun, normally people would take a good **aim**. However, if someone just lays there but get shot, then he/she might be really unlucky. "Get dissed" (lay there and got shot) indicates that someone didn't do anything and being low-key, yet was **mentioned** in other people's conversation. And the content, quite frequently, is not something pleasant. The **gossip** news, for instance, loves to talk about celebrities' private life, for example, the pop star ,Taylor Swift, who **is accustomed to** put her ex in her songs, is always under **spotlight** to get dissed. One time a guy said he would never date Taylor because he doesn't want to be written in her song. Be careful thought that in Chinese, this saying isn't necessarily with negative meaning, yet in English "get dissed" is more or less close to talking behind someone's back. It is popular and be careful to distinguish these two.

※發信站：「鄉民這樣說」實業坊(ptt.cc) 來自 140.115.208.44
※文章網址：https://www.ptt.cc/bbs/PttNewhand/M.1452581219.A.FAF.

→ **Ryan:** You know, Kim got dissed today in class and she's really pissed.

雷恩：你知道嗎？今天上課的時候，金躺著也中槍，她超不爽的。

推 **Billy:** What happened?

比利：怎麼回事？

→ **Ryan:** Mr. White told Zoe that if she doesn't put more attention on her grade, she'd end up working as a barista in Starbucks like Kim.

雷恩：懷特先生告訴柔伊，如果她不重視分數，以後就會跟金一樣在星巴克當咖啡師。

推 **Billy:** Wow, that's bad. Did she lose it?

比利：天啊，太慘了。她有發飆嗎？

→ **Ryan:** Nah, but she slammed the door pretty hard after class.

雷恩：沒有，但下課後她關門超大力的。

推 **Billy:** Gosh, that was hell of a thing that Mr. White said. That must be intense.

比利：夭壽，懷特先生真敢講。也太激烈了吧。

單字加油站

單字	詞性	中譯
1. aim	v.	瞄準
2. mention	v.	提及
3. gossip	n.	八卦
4. be accustomed to	ph.	習慣於
5. spotlight	n.	聚光燈

倍斯特實業坊〉 看版 BESTBOOK_Unit 4-15 也是醉了

作者 鄉民英文原來是醬！Internet Slang on PTT

標題 也是醉了 At a loss for words

醉倒的人往往頭暈目眩、站都站不穩，這句「也是醉了」就是代表某人事物太誇張，讓自己無言以對，很想乾脆昏倒。通常用在對一個人或一件事物極度不認同，或是覺得太過可笑、幾乎到懶得吐槽的地步。英文可表現相同意境的片語有「無言以對」(at a loss for words)、「無話可說」(speechless)等等，都有狀況太誇張，令人無法接受的意思。除了描述一個人或事物愚蠢到讓人受不了，如果事情發展「超展開」、令人難以置信，也可以說自己「醉了」。

MP3 080

Getting drunk means feeling **dizzy** and unable to walk in line. The Chinese slang "I am drunk（我也是醉了）" takes the spirit from it. What it actually means, is that something or somebody is way out of control, to the extent that makes you speechless and feel like **fainting**. The idiom is used to describe an **ultimate** disapproval condition to something or somebody, sometimes too silly to even react to. In English, similar expression includes "I'm **speechless**." or "I'm at a loss for words". Both indicate that the situation is so ridiculous that one refuses or unable to **accept** it. Other than describing a person or a situation, if something turns out to have an unexpected result, one might also say that he/she is at a loss for words.

※發信站：「鄉民這樣說」實業坊(ptt.cc) 來自 140.115.208.44

※文章網址：https://www.ptt.cc/bbs/PttNewhand/M.1452581219.A.FAF.

→ **Ryan:** The NBA game last night was epic. Never seen Lakers get slaughtered by Magic.

雷恩：昨晚的 NBA 球賽有夠誇張，從沒看過湖人被魔術痛宰。

→ **Kim:** Yeah, especially the last two minutes. I couldn't believe that the ball just didn't hit the basket.

金：對啊，尤其是最後兩分鐘，真不敢相信沒進半球。

→ **Ryan:** Yeah. I was pinching myself because that was outrageous!

雷恩：我狂捏自己，因為實在是太扯了！

→ **Kim:** Dude, I was at a loss for words you know? Magic beats Lakers? Come on!

金：老天，我也是醉了好不好，魔術贏湖人？天哪。

→ **Ryan:** Maybe I'll switch to tennis last time, so I won't get too stunned.

雷恩：下次我看網球賽好了，才不會太受驚。

→ **Kim:** That's what makes it so interesting though!

金：但這就是樂趣所在啊！

單字加油站

單字	詞性	中譯
1. dizzy	adj.	暈眩的
2. faint	v.	昏厥
3. ultimate	adj.	終極的
4. speechless	adj.	目瞪口呆的
5. accept	v.	接受

倍斯特實業坊〉 看版 BESTBOOK_Unit 4-16 ㄈㄈ尺	
作者	鄉民英文原來是醬！Internet Slang on PTT
標題	ㄈㄈ尺 Cross Culture Romance

ㄈㄈ尺曾經在 PTT 上掀起一波熱烈的討論，雖然一開始ㄈㄈ尺被大肆批評，但近年來對台灣人來說與一個外國人交往、結婚，好像代表著可愛的混血小孩、出國旅行美景和接觸異國文化，是部分的台灣人心生嚮往的一種生活方式，但有人支持，也有人反對，因為現在也有越來越多這樣的例子，漸漸變成一個網路上流行的話題。但是在英文中，Cross Cultural Romance (異國戀) 不是一個常用的單字，在西方社會，一個比較常見的單字是「interracial romance/interracial relationship」(跨種族戀愛)，指的是黑人與白人間，不同種族間的戀愛，是常被討論和出現在小說、電影中的一個題材。

MP3 081

「ㄈㄈ尺」has once have a serious discussion on the Taiwanese forum PTT. Although it is **criticized** by many people in the first place, dating the foreigners and even the marriage with the foreigners seem **indicate** cute foreign babies, beautiful pictures abroad and a kind of contacting with the **exotic** cultures. Some netizens support and some are against 「ㄈㄈ尺」, and there are more cross cultural romance couples recently and gradually becomes a hot topic on the forum. In English, "Cross culture romance" is not a common word. In Western word, people use "interracial (跨種族的) romance/interracial **relationship**", which is a common term to describe the romance between the couple with the difference **races**, mostly are the black and the white, appears often as the topics of the novels and TV series.

※發信站：「鄉民這樣說」實業坊(ptt.cc) 來自 140.115.208.44
※文章網址：https://www.ptt.cc/bbs/PttNewhand/M.1452581219.A.FAF.

→ **Ryan**：Do you ever image about cross cultural romance? You know like date a foreigner.

雷恩：你有曾經想過談一段異國戀愛嗎？

推 **Kim**：No, I don't. But I know it's a hot topic on PTT. There are thousands of posts about this topic online. How about you?

金：不，我沒有。我知道這是一個在 PTT 上很紅的話題。上面有幾千篇有關這個主題的 po 文。你會想要一段異國戀情嗎？

→ **Ryan**：Oh, I like the foreigner girls because I think they all look cute.

雷恩：噢，我喜歡外國女生，因為她們都長得很可愛。

推 **Kim**： Come on. I don't want to date a foreign guy because I afraid there will be culture shock between us if we are really into a relationship. I am a more conservative person and there will be a lot of problems.

金：又來了。我不想要跟外國男生約會，如果我們真的開始交往的話，我怕會有文化衝擊出現。我比較保守，我想這樣會有很多問題出現。

單字加油站

單字	詞性	中譯
1. criticize	v.	批評
2. indicate	v.	暗示 表明
3. exotic	adj.	異國的
4. relationship	n.	關係 交往關係
5. race	n.	種族

倍斯特實業坊〉看版 BESTBOOK_Unit 4-17 lol

作者	鄉民英文原來是醬！Internet Slang on PTT
標題	「lol」英文的 XD

一開始「lol」是 laugh out loud（大笑）的縮寫，在傳簡訊的時候，好讓使用者省下打字的功夫。以前只要有人說了好笑的話，回覆 lol 絕對無誤，但是現在 lol 不一定還保有「好笑」的成分。反之，lol 成了一種尷尬狀況中的固定回應語，不知道要回什麼就打個 lol，已經變成表情圖示的一種。如果有人想結束對話，他可能會禮貌性地發一個表情圖示，然後直接神隱消失不見，「lol」跟台灣人常用的「XD」有異曲同工之妙。XD 看起來是一張大笑的臉，但現在也未必只在「好好笑」的場合使用。

MP3 082

Originally, "lol" is the **abbreviation** of Laugh Out Loud, applied when texting so that the user doesn't have to text so many words. It was once the answer when someone says something **entertaining,** and you "lol" them. These days, however, lol doesn't necessarily serve the "laugh" part. Instead, it becomes kind of a responder for those situations where one doesn't really know what to say. It becomes an emoji. If one feels like putting a conversation to the end in a **polite** way, he/she might just type an emoji and friendly disappear. "lol" could be compared with "XD" in Taiwanese term, which **visually** likes a laughing face, doesn't serve its "laughing so hard" part **nowadays** either.

※發信站：「鄉民這樣說」實業坊(ptt.cc) 來自 140.115.208.44
※文章網址：https://www.ptt.cc/bbs/PttNewhand/M.1452581219.A.FAF.

(In an online chatroom)
（在網路聊天室）

→ **BabyBear:** You know what I did yesterday? Take a guess!
寶貝熊：你知道我昨天怎樣嗎？猜猜看！

推 **Butterfly:** No idea. What?
蝴蝶：不知道，怎樣？

→ **BabyBear:** I cut a squid alive to make sushi! It's the freshest! Yaaaaay!
寶貝熊：我把烏賊活生生大卸八塊做壽司！超新鮮的！耶！

推 **Butterfly:** lol. Yeah sashimi's the best.
蝴蝶：哈哈，是喔，生魚片最讚。

→ **BabyBear:** I even shoot a video just for that! Check out my YouTube channel! I've already got 4 thumbs up and you're gonna make it 5!
寶貝熊：我還特地拍了個影片欸！看看我的 YouTube 頻道！已經四個人按讚了，你去當第五個吧！

推 **Butterfly:** Lol, that's badass. Well, I'm gonna go. Till next time. Bye.
蝴蝶：不錯喔。我要閃了，下次再聊，掰。

單字加油站

單字	詞性	中譯
1. abbreviation	n.	縮寫
2. entertaining	adj.	好笑的
3. polite	adj.	有禮貌的
4. visually	adv.	看起來地
5. nowadays	adv.	現今

倍斯特實業坊〉看版 BESTBOOK

熱門看板	分類看板

PART

05 → 英文鄉民英語

倍斯特實業坊〉看版 BESTBOOK_Unit 5-1 XOXO

作者 鄉民英文原來是醬！Internet Slang on PTT

標題 XOXO 親親抱抱

近來常看到信件結尾，在署名旁加上 xoxo，第一眼看到，不免納悶這是什麼謎樣符號，但只要從形象的角度來看，就不難猜出 xoxo 的含義。X 字母本身的樣子，就像一個人雙腳交叉著環抱另一個人。而圓潤的圓形 O，則像兩人彼此親吻。只要運用一點想像力，其實 xoxo 就像兩個人熱情擁吻。xoxo 常用在喜愛或想表達愛意的對象身上，網路打字可以用，信件署名時也可以用，不想用 xoxo 的話，老派一點的做法是在信件末尾加上「愛你喔，OOO」或「想著你，XXX」。

MP3 083

It has become more or less common these days that xoxo be part of the signature at the end of a letter. Although it may seem to be a **mysterious** symbol at first sight, xoxo can be easily understood when looking at it in a **physical**-mimicking point of view. X, as the **alphabet** depicts itself, looks like a person crossing legs with arms around one another. O, the perfect round, looks like the two kissing each other. With a little **imagination**, xoxo portraits two people hugging and kissing **passionately**. Thus, the term is used towards whomever one loves and wants to show affection to. It may appear in online texting or at the end of a letter. Either way is pretty common. If you feel awkward to use xoxo, try the old-fashioned way to add “with love, OOO” or “thinking of you, XXX” at the end of a letter.

※發信站：「鄉民這樣說」實業坊(ptt.cc) 來自 140.115.208.44
※文章網址：https://www.ptt.cc/bbs/PttNewhand/M.1452581219.A.FAF.
(Judy and Ryan are texting on their phone.)
（茱蒂和雷恩互傳訊息）

→ **Judy:** So jealous of you. Graduates' ain't got finals.
茱蒂：好羨慕你，研究生沒有期末考。

推 **Ryan:** Woa, watch it. You don't wanna know what's it like to be me.
雷恩：喂，話別說得太早，妳不知道我有多忙。

→ **Judy:** What? You got bigger stuff on your plate?
茱蒂：是喔？有比我忙嗎？

推 **Ryan:** Let's talk about that next time. Good luck!
雷恩：下次再聊吧，加油囉。

→ **Judy:** ooxx, bye.
茱蒂：愛你喔，掰。

單字加油站

單字	詞性	中譯
1. mysterious	adj.	神秘的
2. alphabet	n.	字母
3. physical	adj.	物理上的
4. imagination	n.	想像力
5. passionately	adv.	熱情地

倍斯特實業坊〉看版 BESTBOOK_Unit 5-2 Worth one's salt

作者 鄉民英文原來是醬！Internet Slang on PTT

標題 Worth one's salt 稱職能幹

「worth one's salt」這個片語來源追溯回以前鹽巴還被視為奢侈品的年代，跟現在不同的是，以前的人要取得今日的必需品鹽巴，有時需要花費很大的功夫。只有所謂的特權階級或有特殊成就的人，才能享受鹽巴的滋味。因此可想而知 worth one's salt 的意思是一個人努力工作取得好成果，很稱職能幹的意思。簡單來講，worth one's salt 就是 worth one's salary（付錢請他很值得）。另一方面，如果你已經在工作上勞心勞力，卻沒得到相對的肯定，也可以說自己「not being paid enough」，拿的錢不夠多啦！

MP3 084

The term "worth one's salt" could be traced back to the time where salt is a **luxury** goods. Unlike today, **ancient** civilization doesn't usually get their hands on what is considered a **necessity** of life: salt. As a result, only those who were privileged or pay their efforts, so to speak, could be awarded with salt. As one can imagine, "worth one's salt" **thereby** means that someone works their ass off and have well-accomplished in what they're doing. Simply put, "worth one's salt" equals to "worth one's salary". On the other hand, if you think you've put tears and soul in your work, yet unfortunately is not being **recognized**, you can say that you're "not being paid enough".

※發信站：「鄉民這樣說」實業坊(ptt.cc) 來自 140.115.208.44
※文章網址：https://www.ptt.cc/bbs/PttNewhand/M.1452581219.A.FAF.

→ **Judy:** Did you see Kim the other day? She was running around getting stuff done. She doesn't take a break!

茱蒂：你之前有注意過金嗎？今天她一直忙上忙下，都沒有休息欸！

推 **Billy:** Yeah, she'd be on her feet all day. She doesn't complain.

比利：對啊，一整天她連坐下都沒有，而且毫無怨言。

→ **Judy:** She totally worth her salt you know? Maybe she needs a raise.

茱蒂：她真的超稱職的，真該給她加薪。

推 **Billy:** Well, I don't know about that. Our boss is not that of a money-giver. But she is really a great person to work with.

比利：不知道欸，我們老闆應該是沒那麼大方，但跟她一起上班真的很愉快。

→ **Judy:** I know. She always gets our back. I wish everybody that works here is just like her.

茱蒂：對啊，她很罩。希望每個在這裡上班的人都跟她一樣。

單字加油站

單字	詞性	中譯
1. luxury	adj.	奢侈的
2. ancient	adj.	古代的
3. necessity	n.	必需品
4. thereby	adv.	因此
5. recognize	v.	認同；認可

倍斯特實業坊〉看版 BESTBOOK_Unit 5-3 Conversational blue balls	
作者	鄉民英文原來是醬！Internet Slang on PTT
標題	Conversational blue balls 吊人胃口

「Conversational blue balls」（對話藍球）是指某一個人提起一個有趣的話題後，在講出重點前硬生生轉移話題，而且不解釋這一個話題真正想表達的意思，這種吊人胃口的狀態就叫 conversational blue ball。「Blue ball」藍球的含義其實還挺粗俗的，意思是男性勃起後無法以高潮收場的難受狀態。就像對話硬生生被切斷，讓人很難受，這種狀況也常發生在打字聊天。因為線上聊天不會看到本人，如果對話開始變得奇怪，有的人就會選擇已讀不回，直接放著訊息不看。雖然很痛苦，但這也算是另類的吊人胃口吧！

MP3 085

"Conversational blue balls" refers to the situation when someone brings up an interesting topic, yet right before the funny part he/she drops it and never comes back to the answer. It just keeps you **suspended**. That's what a conversational blue ball does. The term "blue ball" is a rather dirty expression, indicating the condition after a man erected but is unable to finish with **orgasm**. Blue balls here, therefore, represent the funny emotion one feels after a topic has been dropped **abruptly**. This happens when you are texting. Since people don't see each other face to face while online texting, if the conversation turns awkward, some just **opt** to disappear, leaving your message unread. That, **painfully** but truthfully, is another conversational blue ball.

※發信站：「鄉民這樣說」實業坊(ptt.cc) 來自 140.115.208.44
※文章網址：https://www.ptt.cc/bbs/PttNewhand/M.1452581219.A.FAF.

→ **Kim:** Billy gave me a conversational blue ball the other day. It really sucks.

金：比利昨天話講一半，真的很討人厭。

推 **Ryan:** What happened?

雷恩：怎麼回事？

→ **Kim:** He asked if I had a boyfriend, I said no, then he just switched topic.

金：他問我有沒有男朋友，我說沒有，然後他就轉移話題。

推 **Ryan:** That's awful. Maybe he has a crush on you?

雷恩：太糟糕了吧。說不定他煞到妳了？

→ **Kim:** I don't know! I mean he asked me out several times, but he just seems to have many female friends!

金：可能吧！他是有約我出去過很多次，但他好像有很多女性朋友。

推 **Ryan:** You wonder if you are just one of his ordinary friends? Yeah, that'd really suck.

雷恩：妳怕自己只是他眾多閨蜜之一嗎？對啦，那樣就真的太爛了。

單字加油站

單字	詞性	中譯
1. keep someone suspended		使人提心吊膽/好奇
2. orgasm	n.	高潮
3. abruptly	adv.	突然
4. opt	v.	選擇
5. painfully	adv.	痛苦地

倍斯特實業坊〉看版 BESTBOOK_Unit 5-4 Jump the couch

作者	鄉民英文原來是醬！Internet Slang on PTT
標題	Jump the couch 脫軌

正常人應該不會在沙發上蹦蹦跳，除非你想把沙發弄壞。要是有人在沙發上跳來跳去，他要不是個小孩子，要不就是腦筋出問題了。Jump the couch（跳沙發）的意思，應該不難猜一沒錯，就是行為脫序、脫軌。它源自阿湯哥(Tom Cruise)在美國脫口秀名人歐普拉(Oprah)的節目上在沙發上跳上跳下，藉此表達自己對愛人凱蒂(Katie Holmes)的熱烈情意。因此，有人也用這個片語表達向某人示愛的舉動，下次再看到有人做出令人瞠目結舌的舉動，不妨叫他別再「跳沙發」了！

MP3 086

Normally, people wouldn't jump the couch **unless** you want to break it. If somebody does jump the couch, either he is a child or is losing his mind. Get the meaning of "jumping the couch" now? Yes, it is to depict someone's acting **insane**. The expression went wild after Tom Cruise took a step and jumped the couch on American famous talk show host Oprah's TV show in order to express his **affection** towards his loving wife Katie Holmes. Therefore, some also refer to this saying as to display their affection to one another. Next time someone acts absurdly, try to tell he/she stopping jumping the couch!

※發信站：「鄉民這樣說」實業坊(ptt.cc) 來自 140.115.208.44
※文章網址：https://www.ptt.cc/bbs/PttNewhand/M.1452581219.A.FAF.

→ **Judy:** You know, Billy is actually a terrible drinker.

茱蒂：妳知道嗎？比利的酒品很差。

推 **Kim:** How so? I seldom see him drink. I thought he may not drink at all.

金：有嗎？我很少看他喝酒，我還以為他是不喝酒的人欸。

→ **Judy:** He always jumps the couch after he is drunk! That's why.

茱蒂：他喝醉總會做出脫序行為，所以才很少喝啊！

推 **Kim:** Really? Hit me with an example.

金：是喔？說個例子來聽聽。

→ **Judy:** Last time we got drunk together, he nearly stripped down in the pub! I had to force him to go into the cab or he would have slept there half-naked.

茱蒂：上次我們一起買醉，他差點在酒吧脫得一乾二淨！我得把他強押進計程車，否則他會半裸的睡在那裡。

推 **Kim:** Damn, that's wild. I wish I were there.

金：天啊，真狂野，真想看。

單字加油站

單字	詞性	中譯
1. normally	adv.	通常
2. unless		除非
3. insane	adj.	愚蠢、荒唐的
4. affection	n.	情意
5. absurdly	adv.	荒謬地

倍斯特實業坊〉看版 BESTBOOK_Unit 5-5 In a nutshell

作者　鄉民英文原來是醬！Internet Slang on PTT

標題　**In a nutshell 簡而言之**

In a nutshell「在果仁之中」是什麼意思？乍看之下，這好像是某種跟核果有關的料理，但其實這一個片語跟食物無關，反而是「簡而言之」的意思。試想一顆核桃果，外表看似樸實無華，裡頭打開卻有小小宇宙，這就是「in a nutshell」被拿來當作「長話短說」的原因。In a nutshell 通常放在句子開頭，用來省略落落長的前因後果。跟「簡而言之」、「長話短說」意思相近的片語很多，包括「simply put」、「in short」、「by and large」和「in summary」等等，這些詞也都是放在句子開頭。只要一說這些片語，別人就知道你有很多心路歷程，但直接跳過講重點囉！

MP3 087

What does "in a nutshell" possibly mean on earth? At first sight, it may seem to be a dish or **cuisine** associated with nuts, which in fact has nothing to do with any food. This expression means "making a long story short". Think about a walnut. The nut itself has a **modest appearance**, while on the inside there's a whole little **universe**. That is probably why this phrase has been referring to telling story in fewer words. Typically, the term "in a nutshell" appears at the beginning of a sentence, for the purpose of **omitting** long and drastic why and why not. There are tons of similar expressions, including "simply put", "in short", "by and large" and "in summary". These phrases are positioned at the beginning of a sentence. Once you say it, people know that you are skipping the hard-to-describe process and getting to the point!

※發信站：「鄉民這樣說」實業坊(ptt.cc) 來自 140.115.208.44

※文章網址：https://www.ptt.cc/bbs/PttNewhand/M.1452581219.A.FAF.

→ **Kim:** I can't believe Billy can go so wild after he let loose of himself!

金：真不敢相信比利喝醉後這麼狂野！

推 **Judy:** I'm telling you, girl, never judge a book with its cover. Or more likely, never judge a man before he gets drunk.

茱蒂：妹子，告訴妳，千萬別以貌取人。這麼說吧，男人沒喝醉之前，千萬別輕易下斷案。

→ **Kim:** That's mind-blowing. How am I gonna know if a man is okay to be with? I can't get them drunk on the first date. Or all the time.

金：太誇張了，這樣我哪知道可以跟誰交往？我又不能第一次約會就把對方灌醉，或老是把他們灌醉。

推 **Judy:** In a nutshell, don't pour your heart out too easily. That way you don't get hurt.

茱蒂：簡單來說，別輕易付出真心，這樣才不會讓自己受傷。

單字加油站

單字	詞性	中譯
1. cuisine	n.	菜餚
2. modest	adj.	簡樸的
3. appearance	n.	外表
4. universe	n.	宇宙
5. omit	v.	省略

倍斯特實業坊〉看版 BESTBOOK_Unit 5-6 Go nuts

作者　鄉民英文原來是醬！Internet Slang on PTT

標題　Go nuts 起肖

又一個跟堅果有關的片語，而這次也不意外地跟食物沒有關係。「Go nuts」到底是什麼意思？想像一下奇奇蒂蒂兩隻花栗鼠，看到橡實肯定眼冒愛心，說不定還會上演一齣堅果爭奪戰。「Go nuts」就是取「雞飛狗跳」的意境，形容一個人瘋掉的意思。類似的用法還有「Go bananas」，不難想像，猴子搶奪香蕉肯定也和平不到哪裡去吧？所以「Go bananas」也有類似的意思。這些片語不一定是指生氣，也有可能是被別人煩到受不了。下次叫別人走開別煩我，可以說「Stop bugging me!」，別像蟲一樣惹我發飆！

MP3 088

Another term about nut, and unsurprisingly, this time also has nothing to do with food. What exactly does "go nuts" mean? Just imagine the two **chipmunk**s Chip and Dale, when they see an acorn, most likely they'd be shooting out beams of hearts from their eyes, not to mention the fight they'd have in order to get the **prize**. That's right, "go nuts" takes from the chaotic situation to describe one losing his mind. Same expression includes "go bananas". It goes without saying that when two monkeys fighting for a banana, the **scene** wouldn't be so **peaceful**. Thus, "go bananas" also indicates aguy goes crazy. These phrases don't necessary refer to being a guy. Sometimes it's just impatience that plays the **trick**. If you want to tell others to leave you alone, try saying "stop bugging me!". And yes, bugs are annoying.

※發信站：「鄉民這樣說」實業坊(ptt.cc) 來自 140.115.208.44

※文章網址：https://www.ptt.cc/bbs/PttNewhand/M.1452581219.A.FAF.

→ **Billy:** Hi Judy, have you heard back from Kim?

比利：嗨，茱蒂，妳有聽金說了嗎？

推 **Judy:** Am I supposed to hear anything from her? What are you talking about?

茱蒂：我應該從她那裡聽說什麼事嗎？你在說什麼？

→ **Billy:** You know, you are her bestie. I figure she may let out some of her feeling...to you.

比利：因為妳是她的好閨蜜，我想說她可能會跟妳…說一些心事。

推 **Judy:** Dude, if you want to know her feeling, why not go straight to her and ask?

茱蒂：老兄，如果你想知道她的感覺，何不直接問她本人？

→ **Billy:** I can't! I am afraid that she'll turn me down. Would you go ask her for me, please?

比利：我不行！我怕會被她拒絕。妳可以幫我問嗎？拜託啦？

推 **Judy:** Just leave me alone, will you? You're gonna make me go nuts.

茱蒂：別煩我了行不行，我快被你搞到起肖了。

單字加油站

單字	詞性	中譯
1. chipmunk	n.	花栗鼠
2. prize	n.	大獎
3. scene	n.	畫面
4. peaceful	adj.	和平的
5. trick	n.	把戲

倍斯特實業坊〉 看版 BESTBOOK_Unit 5-7 In the soup

作者 鄉民英文原來是醬！Internet Slang on PTT

標題 **In the soup 騎虎難下、進退兩難**

聽到別人說「I'm in the soup!」（我在湯裡！）時，別懷疑，你沒聽錯。不過請注意，他們可不是真的快要溺死在湯裡，其實他們說的是自己惹上麻煩了。這個片語的來由已不可考，大概是在十九世紀時出現的，類似的用法有「in hot water」、「in deep water」或一聽就知道不妙的「in deep shit」。「In hot water」跟中文成語「水深火熱」不謀而合，不管在哪一個國家，惹上麻煩都跟泡在滾燙的水裡一樣讓人難受。

MP3 089

When you hear people say "I'm in the soup!" Don't doubt yourself, you didn't hear it wrong. Be **aware**, though, that they are not **drowning** in the soup as you might imagine. What they actually mean is that they are in trouble. The origin remains **unknown**, but it's probably around somewhere in the 19th century. Similar expressions include "in hot water", "in deep water" or an even more **obvious** one: in deep shit. The saying "in hot water" correspond to a Chinese term "water deep 'n hot"(水深火熱). After all, no matter which country you are in, being in trouble do feel like bathing in **unbearable** hot water.

※發信站：「鄉民這樣說」實業坊(ptt.cc) 來自 140.115.208.44
※文章網址：https://www.ptt.cc/bbs/PttNewhand/M.1452581219.A.FAF.

→ **Ryan:** Hey bro! Heard you have feelings for Kim. Have you made up your mind to talk to her?

雷恩：老兄，聽說你對金有意思，你準備跟她告白了嗎？

推 **Billy:** I didn't tell her. Instead, I stalked her.

比利：我沒跟她告白，反而跟蹤了她。

→ **Ryan:** What? That's messed up! What are you thinking? That's gonna freak her out!

雷恩：啥？那樣很糟糕欸！你在想什麼啊？她肯定嚇到花容失色！

推 **Billy:** Yeah, I wasn't thinking. I just planned on following her home, making sure she's safe. Unfortunately, she spotted me and ran away screaming.

比利：對啊，我沒想太多。本來我只想跟著她回家，確定她平安無事，想不到被她發現了，結果她尖叫著跑掉。

→ **Ryan:** That's really bad. Did she recognize you though?

雷恩：太糟了，但她有發現是你嗎？

推 **Billy:** Yeah, that's why I'm so depressed. I am in the soup right now.

比利：有啊，所以我才這麼沮喪。這下我真的倒大楣了。

單字加油站

單字	詞性	中譯
1. aware	adj.	知道的
2. drown	v.	溺水
3. unknown	adj.	未知的
4. obvious	adj.	明顯的
5. unbearable	adj.	無法忍受的

倍斯特實業坊〉看版 BESTBOOK_Unit 5-8 TBT

作者 鄉民英文原來是醬！Internet Slang on PTT

標題 **TBT 懷舊星期四**

TBT 是懷舊星期四 Throwback Thursday 的首字母縮寫字，這個原創節日是從 Instagram、推特(Twitter)或臉書(Facebook)等社群媒體上開始流行的，由一群使用者在每週四上傳老照片帶動風潮。剛開始這只是一股懷舊運動，人們想藉此重溫以前的重要時刻。照片往往會加上#TBT 或 #throwbackthursday 等標籤，藉由把照片連結到整個標籤底下，順勢增加自己帳號的人氣。現在這股風潮已經不僅限於每週四，無論何時何地，想上傳照片的人隨時都可上傳。有趣的是除了懷舊星期四，現在甚至還衍生出懷舊星期五呢！

MP3 090

TBT is the **acronym** of Throwback Thursday. This original holiday was first seen on social media and is getting popular, such as Instagram, Twitter or Facebook, by a bunch of users who start posting photos of good old days on every Thursday. At the beginning, it is just kind of **nostalgic** trend where people try to **relive** their **memorable** moments. The photos are usually **accompanied** by hashtag #TBT or #throwbackthursday, to which one increases the popularity of their account by putting the photos in the feed. Now "#TBT" does not only take place on Thursdays. It can happen whenever and wherever one wishes it to happen. Funny enough, apart from Throwback Thursday, there is even Flashback Friday.

※發信站：「鄉民這樣說」實業坊(ptt.cc) 來自 140.115.208.44
※文章網址：https://www.ptt.cc/bbs/PttNewhand/M.1452581219.A.FAF.

→ **Ryan:** Is this the picture that you and Kim at Judy's birthday last year?
雷恩：那不是你和金去年在茱蒂生日派對上的合照嗎？

推 **Billy:** Yeah, I'm just posting on my Facebook. I miss the laugh we had.
比利：對啊，我要上傳臉書，真懷念以前的美好時光。

→ **Ryan:** Dude, are you insane? You have mutual friends, she's gonna see it!
雷恩：老兄，你腦子進水啦？你們有共同朋友欸，她會看到的啦！

推 **Billy:** I want her to see. Maybe she'll recall how close we were and forget about me being creepy.
比利：我就是要她看到啊，也許她會因此想起以前我們多親近，然後忘記我的詭異舉動。

→ **Ryan:** No, you can't do that. Here, let me delete it.
雷恩：不，你不能上傳。拿來，我幫你刪掉照片。

推 **Billy:** No, it's done, and I hashtag #TBT. Haha, she's gonna love it!
比利：不行，我已經傳好了，還標籤#TBT 呢。哈哈，她一定很愛！

單字加油站

單字	詞性	中譯
1. acronym	n.	首字母縮寫字
2. nostalgic	adj.	懷舊的
3. relive	v.	重生
4. memorable	adj.	難忘的
5. accompany	v.	伴隨

倍斯特實業坊〉 看版 BESTBOOK_Unit 5-9 Ootd

作者	鄉民英文原來是醬！Internet Slang on PTT
標題	Ootd 今日穿搭

「Ootd」是 Outfit of Today（今日穿搭）的第一個字母縮寫。想也知道，目的就是告訴別人自己穿什麼。如果你想讓朋友驚艷或增加追蹤數，千萬別忘了在一身完美行頭的照片底下標記#ootd。在社群媒體氾濫的現代，人們重視自己的程度可說是前所未見。從身上的衣服到盤中飧，每個小細節都不能忽略，如此才能拍出完美照片。故此，除了 ootd，網路上也開始流行其他標籤。#shoefie 就是其中之一，意思是給鞋子拍自拍照。也許聽起來很可笑，但如果你想在社群媒體中成為網路紅人，學個一兩招總是沒壞處。

MP3 091

Ootd is the acronym of Outfit of Today. Quite literally, it is an indication of what you're wearing today. If you want to wow your friends and increase your followers, adding hashtag #ootd with your **stunning** outfit is a must-do. As social media taking over the **cyber world**, people pay more attention to what they're doing and themselves more than ever. From what one's wearing to their food in the plates, every little **detail** must be taken care of in order to have the perfect photo shoot. As a result, other than ootd, there are all kinds of hashtags, #shoefie, which refers to a "shoe selfie" is one of them. Maybe it sounds **silly**, but if you want to be one of those Internet celebrities on social media, you've got to know some **gimmick**.

※發信站：「鄉民這樣說」實業坊(ptt.cc) 來自 140.115.208.44
※文章網址：https://www.ptt.cc/bbs/PttNewhand/M.1452581219.A.FAF.

→ **Kim:** Look! The photo I posted just two minutes ago has already got 500+ likes!

金：你看，我兩分鐘前上傳的照片已經超過 500 個讚了！

推 **Ryan:** Good for you, mama! Oh my gosh, you look stunning!

雷恩：妹子，不錯喔！天啊，妳簡直美呆了。

→ **Kim:** Am I? That's fair, though, considering how many photos I shot just to get those perfect five.

金：有嗎？也難怪啦，都不知道拍了幾張才有這五張好看的。

推 **Ryan:** You're dope. Hey, check it out, Billy also got pictures under ootd hashtag.

雷恩：妳美到出水了。喂，妳看，比利在 ootd 標籤下也有照片欸。

→ **Kim:** What? That guy? He is gross...wait, huh, his selfie is actually kind of hot.

金：啥？那傢伙？他超詭異…等等，欸，他的自拍照其實還滿帥的。

推 **Ryan:** Somebody's got some feelings in here. Woo-hoo!

雷恩：有人心動囉，哇嗚！

單字加油站

單字	詞性	中譯
1. stunning	adj.	美得驚人的
2. cyber world	n.	網路世界
3. detail	n.	細節
4. silly	adj.	可笑的
5. gimmick	n.	花招

倍斯特實業坊〉 看版 BESTBOOK_Unit 5-10 The devil is in the details

作者 鄉民英文原來是醬！Internet Slang on PTT

標題 The devil is in the details 魔鬼藏在細節裡

我們都知道魔鬼不是好東西，但藏在細節裡的魔鬼是什麼意思？其實這句話要反過來看，也就是說，細節往往是暗藏玄機的地方。注重細節，就能造就驚人佳績。這句話其實是指一件事可能看起來平實而美好，但那是因為在細節上煞費苦心的緣故，也能用來形容一個人並非無緣無故就成功，而是在很多不為人知的細節上努力，造就出來的成果。另有一句類似的片語「上帝藏在細節裡」，這句話比較偏向警世寓言，用來告誡做事之前應該留心細節。

MP3 092

We all know that devil is not a good thing, but what is devil hidden in the details"? In fact, we should look at this phrase with a different **angle**. What it really means is that people usually don't pay attention to details enough, and those who **nail** on details can bring about huge success. That is to say, something may look **glamorous** and easy to achieve, yet all that **shimmering** appearance is built on hard works behind closed doors. This phrase could also indicate that someone does not achieve their success by accident; they work their ass out for it. Similar expression includes "God's in the details", **whereas** this one is more of a reminder, telling people to mind the details before they start.

※發信站：「鄉民這樣說」實業坊(ptt.cc) 來自 140.115.208.44
※文章網址：https://www.ptt.cc/bbs/PttNewhand/M.1452581219.A.FAF.

→ **Kim:** So, I still can't get over with the stalking stuff...I'm just here for a question.

金：我還沒原諒你跟蹤我，我只是有一個問題想問你。

→ **Kim:** How can your legs look so long and straight and flawless in the picture?

金：為什麼你的腿拍出來總是又長又直又完美？

推 **Billy:** That's all you want to know?

比利：這就是妳想問的事情？

→ **Kim:** Of course! We are Internet celebrities! Photos are lives!

金：對啊！我們是網紅欸！照片就是生命！

推 **Billy:** Okay, here's what you gonna do. Pose at the center of the picture, body slightly lean to the side, camera down.

比利：我教妳。先在照片中央擺姿勢，身體稍微往旁邊靠，相機由下往上。

→ **Kim:** Can't believe that's me! Devil's in the details, isn't it?

金：真不敢相信這是我！魔鬼真的藏在細節裡呢！

單字加油站

單字	詞性	中譯
1. angle	n.	角度
2. nail	v.	成功做到某事
3. glamorous	adj.	迷人的
4. shimmering	adj.	閃閃發光的
5. whereas	conjun.	反之

倍斯特實業坊〉 看版 BESTBOOK_Unit 5-11 Hashtag

作者 鄉民英文原來是醬！Internet Slang on PTT

標題 Hashtag #標籤

簡單來說，網路上的 hashtag，尤其是 hashtag 的發明地 Instagram，是把一則貼文分享給廣大使用者的好方法。只要在#後加上你所希望連結的內容，這一則貼文就會和其他類似主題的貼文連結。舉例來說，在貼文中標註#cafetokyo，附上一張經過精心設計後拍攝的照片，並設為公開，你的貼文就有機會被全世界對這一個主題有興趣的用戶看到，你的貼文就有機會贏得上百人按讚。今天，hashtag 無疑已經成為社群媒體重度使用者的必備神器，hashtag 能帶來更多讚數，而身為一名網紅更多讚數和追蹤數就代表賺更多外快和名氣。想成為時尚潮人嗎？快學學怎麼用 hashtag 吧！

MP3 093

In short, hashtag on the Internet (especially on where's from: Instagram) is a **method** to connect one's post to the rest of **vast** users. Simply by adding # and a topic that you wish to connect to, your post can be found **worldwide** with those users who are interested in this **field** and this topic. For instance, add #cafetokyo with a well-**calculated** and positioned picture, set your account as public then your post suddenly has a chance to get hundreds of likes because your post can be viewed by worldwide users whom are interested in the same topic. Hashtag today has undoubtedly become part of a post if you are a serious social media addict. It can help you to gain more likes which means many followers and more money. Get a hold of how to use hashtag if you want to be one of the coolest kids!

※發信站：「鄉民這樣說」實業坊(ptt.cc) 來自 140.115.208.44
※文章網址：https://www.ptt.cc/bbs/PttNewhand/M.1452581219.A.FAF.

→ **Billy:** There you go! That's a good selfie.
比利：好耶！這張自拍照真好看。

推 **Kim:** I'm gonna post it on Instagram and Facebook. Hashtag #bff #ootd.
金：我要貼到 Instagram 和臉書上，標記#一輩子好友 #今日穿搭。

→ **Billy:** Whoa whoa whoa, wait, since when we become bffs?
比利：喂，等等，我們什麼時候變成一輩子好友了？

→ **Kim:** What? Am I not your best friend?
金：什麼？我不是你最好的朋友嗎？

→ **Billy:** I mean...never mind. Hey, you add hashtag #girlsnightout, too!
比利：我是說…算了。嘿，妳應該順便標記#女子之夜！

推 **Kim:** Shut up! Oh my gosh. We look AWESOME.
金：討厭啦！天啊，我們真的好看到爆。

→ **Billy:** (To himself) I thought we are more than friends...
比利：（自言自語）我以為我們不只是朋友…

單字加油站

單字	詞性	中譯
1. method	n.	方法
2. vast	adj.	廣大的
3. worldwide	adj.	遍及全球的
4. field	n.	領域
5. calculate	v.	計算

倍斯特實業坊〉看版 BESTBOOK_Unit 5-12 Be chill, passive

作者　鄉民英文原來是醬！Internet Slang on PTT

標題　佛系 Be chill, passive

我們都知道佛家有種隨波逐流的生活態度，佛教徒總是與世無爭。對他們來說，人生只是一場由試煉構築而成的修行之旅。最近人們開始拿這種佛家態度來稱呼別人「佛系」，意思是某人對一切不屑一顧。「Chill」這個字不只用來形容某人對凡事都不執著，還能強調他們慢熱型的天性，與「sb's chill」（某人很淡定、很佛系）相反的是「sb's super uptight」（某人超神經質），用來形容什麼都要照表操課的偏執狂。另外，因為「佛系」也有逆來順受的感覺，因此「passive」（被動的）也能用來形容佛系人不努力、不強求、不積極，時候到了自然成功的感受。

MP3 094

We all know that Buddhism bears a sort of go-with-the-stream lifestyle. Buddhists do not argue about anything. Life for them is just like a journey, a series of harsh tests. Nowadays, people start taking this attitude and call upon others to be "buddh-ish", which in other words, is super chill about everything. The word "chill" not only refers to people who insist on nothing, but also means that they have a really calm nature. Opposite from "sb's chill", there is "sb's super uptight", which indicates people who demand everything to be on schedule and upright. Besides, "buddh-ish" people tend to take everything that comes in their way. Thus, one may use "passive" to describe their unwillingness to try and to ask. Typically, they just wait for the good outcome to show up simultaneously.

※發信站：「鄉民這樣說」實業坊(ptt.cc) 來自 140.115.208.44
※文章網址：https://www.ptt.cc/bbs/PttNewhand/M.1452581219.A.FAF.

→ **Kim:** Don't you think Yves is a bit too chill about everything?
金：你覺不覺得伊夫很「佛系」？

推 **Billy:** Yeah, it seems like the whole world is just some crap to him.
比利：對啊，感覺他把一切都看得雲淡風輕。

→ **Kim:** He is super cool, though. One time I forgot my textbook, and he just leaned over and said: "Do you mind?"
金：但他很酷欸。上次我忘記帶課本，他不動聲色的靠過來問我：「要一起看嗎？」

推 **Billy:** Well, I can do that too! I wouldn't mind sharing my book with you.
比利：這我也會啊！我也可以把課本借妳看。

推 **Kim:** There's something about him though. Under that stiff face, I bet something unknown is boiling.
金：但他真的很神秘。在那張撲克臉底下，他肯定有什麼不為人知的秘密。

單字加油站

單字	詞性	中譯
1. lifestyle	n.	生活方式
2. argue	v.	爭論
3. harsh	adj.	嚴苛的
4. nature	n.	天性
5. uptight	adj.	急躁不安的

倍斯特實業坊〉看版 BESTBOOK_Unit 5-13 Smh

作者 鄉民英文原來是醬！Internet Slang on PTT

標題 **Smh 傻眼貓咪**

Smh 是英文「搖搖頭」的縮寫，通常用來表示某人或某事非常令人失望或是很傻氣。這一個詞也帶有一絲對某事感到難以置信，令人詫異到說不出話來的含義。最近網路上很紅的「傻眼貓咪」與 smh 不謀而合，都有覺得某人或一件事情誇張到讓人傻眼的意思。當我們對一個人的舉止感到無可奈何時，常常會翻白眼，翻白眼的英文是「roll one's eyes」。不過，相較於現實生活中常看到的翻白眼，smh 是只在網路上看到的鍵盤用語喔！

MP3 095

Smh is the abbreviation of "shaking my head", **typically** used when somebody or something is **utterly** disappointing or silly. The term also represents a sense of **amazement** when something is way unbelievable to the degree that blows someone's mind. Smh bears a similar usage to a term that goes viral on the Internet these days: "a **face palm** cat " (傻眼貓咪). Both terms convey a message that someone or something's ridiculous outcome has made others speechless. If someone's behavior leads us **impatient**, our typical reaction is to roll our eyes to them. While smh could only be seen in texting and online, rolling one's eyes may appear more frequently in real life.

※發信站：「鄉民這樣說」實業坊(ptt.cc) 來自 140.115.208.44
※文章網址：https://www.ptt.cc/bbs/PttNewhand/M.1452581219.A.FAF.
(In an online chatroom)（在網路聊天室）

→ **Leo:** I don't get fashion. A T-shirt with green stripes costs 300 dollars? Screw me!

獅子座：我真不懂時尚。一件綠色條紋上衣要價 300 美元？有沒有搞錯？

推 **Aquarius:** I know, and the fact that Gucci had someone had-written some random words on their shirt and costs a thousand? I say let them have at it!

水瓶座：對啊，Gucci 只是叫某個路人甲在衣服上隨便寫個字，就賣一千美元！誰會買啊？

→ **Leo:** I wonder what kind of dummies would waste their money on it.

獅子座：不知道哪種傻蛋會浪費錢去買。

推 **Pisces:** What's up guys? I just bought a new pair of boots in Calvin Klein and it costs only 500 dollars!

雙魚座：你們好嗎？我剛買了一雙 CK 的靴子，只要 500 美元欸！

→ **Leo:** Smh.

獅子座：傻眼貓咪。

單字加油站

單字	詞性	中譯
1. typically	adv.	典型地
2. utterly	adv.	徹底地
3. amazement	n.	詫異
4. facepalm	n.	捂臉的動作；傻眼
5. impatient	adj.	不耐的

國家圖書館出版品預行編目(CIP)資料

鄉民英文原來是醬！/陳怡歆、柯志儒著--
初版. -- 臺北市：倍斯特,2019.05面；公分.--
（文法/生活英語系列；010）
ISBN 978-986-97075-6-5（平裝附光碟）
1.英語 2.讀本

805.18 108004901

文法/生活英語 010

鄉民英文原來是醬！(附MP3)

初　　版　2019年5月
定　　價　新台幣380元

作　　者　陳怡歆、柯志儒
出　　版　倍斯特出版事業有限公司
發 行 人　周瑞德
電　　話　886-2-8245-6905
傳　　真　886-2-2245-6398
地　　址　23558 新北市中和區立業路83巷7號4樓
E-mail　best.books.service@gmail.com
官　　網　www.bestbookstw.com
執行總監　齊心瑀
企劃編輯　曾品綺
封面構成　盧穎作
內頁構成　菩薩蠻數位文化有限公司
印　　製　大亞彩色印刷製版股份有限公司

港澳地區總經銷　泛華發行代理有限公司
地　　址　香港新界將軍澳工業邨駿昌街7號2樓
電　　話　852-2798-2323
傳　　真　852-3181-3973